# Runner

# Runner

Peter McPhee

James Lorimer & Company Ltd., Publishers
Toronto, 1999

First publication in the United States, 1999

James Lorimer & Company Ltd. acknowledges the support of the Department of Canadian Heritage and the Ontario Arts Council in the development of writing and publishing in Canada. We acknowledge the support of the Canada Council for the Arts for our publishing program.

Cover illustration: Jeff Domm                    Canadä

---

**Canadian Cataloguing in Publication Data**

McPhee, Peter, 1957-
    Runner

ISBN 1-55028-675-X (bound)  ISBN 1-55028-674-9 (pbk.)

I. Title

PS8575.P44R86 1999    jC813'.54    C99-930696-0
PZ7.M35Ru 1999

---

James Lorimer              Distributed in the United States by:
& Company Ltd.,            Orca Book Publishers,
Publishers                 P.O. Box 468
35 Britain Street           Custer, WA USA
Toronto, Ontario           98240-0468
M5A 1R7

Print

*For Elizabeth, our mother.*

*I would like to thank the people who shared their experiences while writing this book — in particular, Janelle, Jan, Tom, and Debby.*

# Chapter 1

"How dare you disobey me again!"

"I told you I'd head downtown after school," Kyle answered. He shifted his weight, trying to get as comfortable as possible on the hard bench as his mother shouted at him from the other end of the telephone line. Tired of their usual conversation, Kyle looked out the cracked window of the phone booth at traffic on 12th Avenue. The night was miserably cold and a light rain had begun turning the pavement black and shiny. As he continued to look out, a pair of teenaged boys, a year or so younger than Kyle, ran into the traffic, causing cars to swerve, skidding on the greasy roads, horns blasting. The boys shot the finger at the drivers, laughing at the havoc they had caused, as they jumped onto the brown grass on the other side of the avenue.

"Are you listening to me?"

"Yeah. I'm listening," Kyle replied. "Look. I told you already. I'll be home in an hour. I just want to check out a couple more places tonight."

"At nearly eleven on a school night? It'll take you an hour just to get home from downtown! I want you to leave right now!"

"And I told you I'm staying here!" Kyle could feel his anger begin to rise. His mother rarely made it home before ten most nights. If he hadn't called, she would have gone straight to bed, thinking he was safe in his own room. From now on, he told himself, I'll just worry about me.

"Now you listen …" his mother began again.

"No!" Kyle shouted back, cutting her off. "You listen to me for once! It's been weeks now and nothing's happened! Maybe you can just sit around waiting, but I'm sick of it!"

"What did you say?" His mother's voice had turned cold now. He knew from experience that he had pushed her past being just angry with him. Kyle looked out the phone booth glass once more, seeing the two boys approach. They looked in, seeing Kyle sitting alone, no one else waiting outside for him.

"Time's up, Marlborough Man," one of the boys said, banging on the glass. He was terribly skinny and wore a short-sleeved shirt under a filthy jean jacket. The arms of the jacket were ripped off and Kyle saw a number of homemade tattoos scarring the boy's thin arms. His partner, equally skinny and with a fringe of neon green hair, began to kick the door methodically with his high boots. Kyle shifted the phone to his other ear, turning away from the boys.

"You aren't the only one in this family who's worried," his mother continued. Her voice was low

2

now and eerily calm. "I work hard to keep a home for us. You seem to think you're the only one whose life's been turned upside down. Let me tell you, I'd trade your life for mine in a second. It'd be nice if all I had to worry about was football practice or which party I had to go to this weekend."

Kyle had heard this speech before and was preparing his own well-rehearsed reply when he was interrupted by a loud crash. He looked up. The green-haired boy had jumped against the booth, his face pushed against the glass and contorted into a grotesque mask, breath and saliva smearing the gritty surface.

"Get the hell away from me!" Kyle shouted angrily, tired of the added annoyance of these two clowns. He kicked the glass for effect.

"Who are you talking to?" his mother asked.

"Look," Kyle said, ignoring the question. "I gotta go!" He still heard his mother's voice as he slammed the phone back on the hook. He zipped up his Marlborough Monarchs team jacket as the bare-armed boy pushed open the door. Kyle knew what he must look like to these boys, now standing over him. His face was round and unlike most of his teammates, still as smooth as a twelve-year-old's. His dark hair was cropped close to the scalp, and Kyle felt this only added to his baby-faced appearance.

"It's about time, Marlborough Man! This is a private phone!"

"A private phone? Really?" Kyle looked at the battered *Telus* phone booth.

3

"Maybe he should pay a fine!" the green-haired boy said as he slid around to the door. Both boys giggled at the idea, as if it was the most original thought they'd ever had.

"Yeah," the other boy said. "Maybe he should give us that jacket."

"Who cares about the jacket? I want cash!"

"I don't think so," Kyle said. He had nearly forgotten the angry conversation with his mother. The two idiots in front of him had given him something else to think about.

"Hey!" the green-haired boy shouted. "Did we ask for your opinion?"

"We're going to take anything we want!" his partner added.

Kyle began to rise slowly from the tiny bench. He saw both boys' eyes grow wider as he stood to his full height. The effect was almost comical. Back in September, when he had tried out for the Monarchs, he had been slightly over six feet. That was only two months ago and he knew he had grown since. The team jacket had arrived only a few days ago and it was too small in the sleeves.

"I think you'd better get out of the way," Kyle said slowly. Both boys backed up as he stepped out of the booth.

"Come on," No-sleeves said. "We got better stuff to do."

Green-hair looked up at Kyle, obviously wondering whether he was worth the effort of robbing. He began to back off as well.

"You better stay away from here," he shouted. "This is our street!"

Kyle laughed at their attempt to save face while running away. He had seen it many times before. In spite of his baby face, he was proud of his size and the effect it had on others. Kyle pulled up the collar of his jacket as he walked into the icy rain, now no more than a drizzle, but still bone-chilling. With a final glance back, to make sure the boys had kept walking, Kyle stepped onto the street. He saw people mill around him as he walked through a park on the corner of 4th Street and 12th Avenue. As he walked, he could see the red sides of the Calgary Tower peer through the office buildings, its lights muted by the thick fog covering the city. Kyle still grinned whenever he noticed it. Compared to the one he had grown up seeing, this tower looked like a Lego toy. Still, he thought, the lights blinking around it gave the city a Christmas feel, even though it was still over a month away.

Kyle walked past the statue of some unknown hero sheltering a small group of kids, huddled together to keep warm. A flame, part of the memorial, burned at the top of a post and a group of kids shoved each other to get close. Graffiti was spray-painted on the side of the statues, on benches, any free surface. Some of it was crude, some beautifully done. Two slogans caught his attention: "Age is the Enemi!" one read. "No the rulz!" read the other. The handwriting on both was perfect, executed in a clean, almost professional way. Completely different than the other hurried scrawls. Kyle wondered what they could possibly mean, other than the fact the writer needed a dictionary.

The face of a young girl seemed to float out of the shadows toward him. He slowed to look and guessed she was no more than eight or nine. An older girl, maybe Meghan's age, stood with her. Both of them were dressed completely in black and the little girl's hands and face were so pale and thin the skin seemed to reflect the weak street light. A dark mark over the girl's upper lip stood out against the surrounding pale skin. It looked like a crooked little moustache. A blood-red moustache. She held up one of those thin hands as the older girl asked him for money.

"Why aren't you at home?" he asked the youngest girl.

The older one swore at him.

"Nice way to talk!" Kyle said, a little shocked by the words coming from such an innocent-looking face. She swore again, with even better effect, before turning away to beg others walking past. Kyle watched her for a moment, wondering what had brought them to this place, then he too turned away. On the south side of 12th Avenue the lights were brighter and the blocks between 4th and 1st Streets were full of bars, pool halls, and cafes. He saw that they were much seedier here than the trendy places along 4th itself. He was proud of how well he was finding his way around such unfamiliar territory.

Music and light poured out of the doors of each place Kyle passed. Most of the inhabitants of the area were teens like him. Unlike him, though, they were ragged and dirty-looking. They looked at him with hollow eyes that dismissed him as an outsider. He pushed his way past a sea of multi-coloured hair, skin-tight clothes, baggy clothes, earrings, and other items of jewellery piercing a wide range of body parts.

Up ahead he saw the sign of the place he had been looking for, a coffee shop called The Koop. It was a hangout for street kids and runaways, or those trying to pretend they were part of the street. As he made his way past a knot of kids piling out of a pool hall, pushed out on a breeze thick with the smell of cigarette smoke and beer, Kyle saw something that made his heart pound.

She stood only a few doors away, pushing back her long, thick hair in a gesture he had seen since childhood. She wore her familiar green and black Thornhill High jacket and one of those goofy, tiny backpacks all the girls seemed to have these days. Protected between her feet was a heavier, much bigger bag. She stood with two other girls, both leaning against a window, smoking and trying to look tough. Kyle picked up his pace, not seeing or caring about the people he shoved aside as he rushed toward Meghan. One of the leaning girls, the tallest one, heard the commotion first, as kids swore at the huge kid pushing through the crowded avenue. She looked at Kyle with an expression that was some-how bored and curious at the same time.

As he began to reach out for Meghan, Kyle saw the other girls begin to stand, seeing at last who he had singled out. Just as Meghan began to turn, Kyle grabbed her by the shoulders and spun her around to face him. That's when his heart lurched again.

It wasn't Meghan.

"What the hell you doin'?" the tall smoker screamed as she stepped forward. The girl Kyle held just looked up at him. She was obviously on something and Kyle saw she was trying to figure out what was happening to her.

"Get your hands off me!" she shouted at last and began to shake herself free. Kyle let go.

"What do you think you're doing?" the girl asked. Her tall friend had begun to move now, cigarette held firmly between her lips, stepping up to Kyle and pushing him hard. He stepped back, feeling stupid and embarrassed at making such a mistake.

"I ... I'm sorry ..." he stammered. "I thought you were someone else!"

"Yeah, right!" the girl replied, "real original!" She pushed him now too, not wanting her friend to outdo her.

"You better take off while you can, jerk," the girl furthest away added, "before we cut off your hands for grabbing her."

Kyle began to apologize again. He hated how he could be so slow sometimes, not thinking fast enough. There must be dozens of other girls with long brown hair wearing Thornhill jackets. How could he have thought it was Meghan? Then his thoughts began to clear. Sure there were other girls wearing that jacket, but they were wandering down Yonge Street back home in Toronto. How many girls wore them on 12th Avenue in Calgary?

He grabbed the girl by the shoulders again, his embarrassment turning to anger. There on the upper right arm he saw the embroidered patch, the name PERRY stitched on it.

"Where'd you get this jacket?"

"Hey! We won't tell you again!" the tallest girl said. "Get your hands off her!"

Kyle turned quickly to the other two, who were starting to move in on him again.

"Back off!" he hissed. For the first time, a glimmer of worry was in their eyes.

"It's my jacket!" the girl said at last.

"No," Kyle said as his voice took the same icy tone he'd inherited from his mother. "Where did you get it?" he asked again.

"I told you! It's mine. They gave me it!"

"Who gave it to you?" Kyle had lifted the girl up, her feet were dangling inches above the sidewalk.

"You're hurting me!" the girl screamed. She wasn't frightened by him, but she seemed to know better than to fight a crazy person.

"Where did you get this jacket?" Kyle shouted again, his voice a little louder.

"Let go of her!" the closest friend screamed. Kyle was vaguely aware that the voices around him had died down, that more people began to surround them, watching the little spectacle he had created.

"I just want to know where she got the jacket!"

"I told you they gave it to me! At Mustard Seed!"

"When?"

The girl shook her head, her face twisted in pain as Kyle's hands dug into her upper arms.

"Tonight! A couple of hours ago!"

Kyle had to think again. He'd heard of Mustard Seed, it was some kind of drop-in centre. He wanted to ask another question when the girl started to scream in anger and kick. Like most of the kids down here, she wore heavy boots, and one kick landed squarely on his shin. He yelled out in pain, and the other girls took their opportunity. They began to kick and punch at him until he let the girl go, to protect himself. He pushed them away and they began to run.

"No! Wait!" he screamed, reaching out for the girl. He grabbed the hem of Meghan's jacket and held on while the girl who now wore it struggled to get free. The taller friend fished around in her purse and pulled out a long, sharp blade, the handle gone, the end wrapped in black tape. She swore at Kyle as she swung the knife at his face. He reacted quickly, moving out of the way just in time, but his balance was off and he slipped on the slick pavement. As he fell he heard a tearing sound and the girl was free. Something small and black fell to the wet concrete. The three girls ran, lost quickly in the crowd.

Kyle, breathless and in pain, looked at his right sleeve. The tall girl's knife had sliced through the outer shell, but hadn't touched his skin. Then he noticed again the black object that lay on the ground inches from him. It was a notebook, coil-bound and battered. Loose, torn pages and bits of scrap paper bulged around the edges, held in place by thick elastic bands. Kyle reached out and grabbed it up, holding it closer to the neon lights from the pool hall. The cover was worn but it still had a carefully printed title page. It read: This is the Diary of Meghan Perry! HANDS OFF!

There in the middle of a busy street, surrounded by other kids, Kyle Perry felt an embarrassing lump in his throat, saw his hands shake as he realized what he held. He had at last found the first piece of the puzzle. He was even more convinced that he would bring his sister home.

# Chapter 2

July 5

Dear Diary,

Are you really supposed to write that? It sounds so lame! Starting anything with "Dear" sounds pretty lame when you think about it. But I suppose it is the proper form and we do want to be proper.

So how should I start my first and only attempt at keeping one of these things? Dear Meghan? Dear Meg? Dear Per? Dear Me?

I kind of like that last one. I'm sure it'll look pretty juvenile when I'm like thirty or something with five kids and worried about my weight and if my husband's really working late at the office and stuff, but right now, who cares? It's me writing this for me. Maybe I'll even turn it into a novel or something. Hopefully I'll actually be a writer by then. So when I'm thirty or something, I'll look back at all of this and laugh? Right? I can hardly wait! So here we go.

Dear Me:

So how've we been? Well, since you ask, things are pretty lousy right now. Mom and Dad finally made it official about a month ago and so here we are, me, Mom, and Kyle living in a lousy three-bedroom house in beautiful northeast Calgary! As I look out my window into the back alley I can see a couple of rednecks (let's call them Billy Bob and Billy Joe) leaning over the hood of a beaten-up pickup, swilling beer and laughing loudly about something they find amusing. Probably planning on ravishing some poor fourteen-year-old girl.

Is it ravish or ravage? Maybe I should ask my brother the A-student (she added sarcastically). He'd probably think it's radish!

Billy Bob down there is actually wearing a cowboy hat! I feel like I'm in the middle of Alabama or something! This can't be Canada, can it?

Just think, only weeks ago I was living the life of a fairly normal teenaged girl in a quietly affluent Toronto suburb (I read that in the *Star*'s homes section). Hanging out at the Eaton Centre, meeting boys, taking old ladies' seats on the subway, meeting boys, doing the usual dumb stuff that a teenaged girl's supposed do (like meeting boys).

(Okay. Since this is my diary and you're supposed to tell the truth, maybe I spent more time *trying* to meet boys than actually meeting them.)

The point is … I was fairly normal. So what if my parents barely spoke, and when they did it was more like shouting? At least they were living in the same (quietly affluent) house. Which in my circle of friends was pretty unusual.

I guess that's what I miss the most. All my friends. I hate the idea of going to a brand new school, being the new kid. And what if they're all hicks like Billy Bob and Billy Joe out there! Am I supposed to start wearing cowboy boots and listening to Garth Brooks? I'd rather be listening to Alanis Morrisette with Emily (and making our parents believe that we don't understand the lyrics).

(Okay! Okay! I've just read the first part over! Boy! I sound like such a snob! I have to try to give people a chance. That's what Mom says all the time. I'll try. Okay? I promise!)

I miss Emily and Carol the most. The last few months we hung out a lot together. I slept at Emily's more than I did my own place. We used to sneak out late at night and just wander the streets, talking and junk. It felt really great, like there were no rules and no parents and we could just do whatever we wanted. The streets are so quiet at night, so peaceful. They're also pretty exciting! Like the time we all went down to Yonge and watched the street people begging and the hookers picking up old guys in big cars. Once we even missed the last subway and had to hitchhike home. That was pretty scary, and the old guy who picked us up was a little creepy. I think he was trying to come on to me. You hear all kinds of stories about weirdos and stuff, but that made it even more exciting.

But that's the past. My future seems to be stuck here alone and friendless and visiting my grandmother. This is another treat mother gave me by moving out here. Reuniting me with my long-lost relatives. My mother used to tell me stories about how she couldn't wait to get out of Calgary, to get away from her family. She left when she was two years older than I am now!

Ever since the breakup and all the problems with Dad, Mom's been talking with Grandma more than ever. They barely talk for over 20 years, and now they're all close again. I don't get it. Why is her mother such a different person than the one she ran away from when she was 16?

She used to be so proud of her stories about how she made it all on her own. How there were still hippies hanging out in Yorkville when she arrived back in the seventies. Big deal. She never mentions the fact that she was lucky enough to find a rich husband. Even if he wasn't all that rich back when they first met. I used to think her stories were so romantic. Now that I'm older, I think I'd never be dumb enough to fall for someone like my dad. Someone who only cares about himself, who doesn't worry about what happens to anyone around him.

In 20-something years she went back to Calgary maybe 10 times, and all she ever did was complain about it. Now we get to see Grandma all the time. It's a real treat going over there. The house smells weird, and Grandma smokes like a chimney and tells me how to dress and to stop wearing make-up and stuff. I hardly know the woman and she thinks she can tell me how to act! It's like I'm in the middle of a bad soap or something!

15

(Okay, okay! She's okay I guess, it's just that it's so weird having her around. It's not like I grew up with her. And she is trying to be nice, she just doesn't get that it's different than when she was my age.)

I guess I'm just mad that Mom lets Grandma talk that way to me. She tries to defend me a little, but she doesn't try all that hard! She caves in to her like she did to Dad and to Kyle whenever they push her enough. If it was me and my husband started taking off with bimbos, I'd take him for everything! That's what Emily's mother did. And she got the house and all kinds of stuff.

Gee, does it sound like I'm feeling sorry for myself? So what? Somebody has to.

Speaking of Kyle, Mom's been bugging Big Brother to spend more time with me. Take me places. She thinks after all that's happened we should be closer. No chance! She thinks we should be like the Brady Bunch and we're more Nightmare on 37th Avenue N.E.! It's a whole different show, Mom!

Kyle and I have barely tolerated each other since I was about four. My dumb jock brother thinks he's too cool to bother with his little sister. And since I dared to embarrass him by getting old enough to attend the same high school, things have got even worse. What's he going to do out here, now that he doesn't have his football team and all his pathetically cool friends to hang out with? I guess I shouldn't ask, he'll probably have everyone running around after him like he always does. Even if he did offer to do stuff with me, I wouldn't go. I have my pride! He's basically treated me like an embarrassment for 10 years so why should I bother with him now?

I suppose I could put up with him if it gets me out of this house and away from Billy Joe and Billy Bob and the rest of my neighbours. I'd like to see the other parts of the city. It can't be nearly as bad as here.

Okay. I'm tired and I've got another exciting day ahead of me tomorrow. My mother has a day off from her new job and she's taking me to the Stampede. She tells me she used to love it when she was my age. She says it's like the CNE except with country music. I can hardly wait!

Bye for now, pardner!

— Meghan

# Chapter 3

Kyle squeezed himself behind the tiny, round table in the cramped kitchen. He carried an empty bowl, a jug of milk, and cereal. The *Calgary Sun*, already open to the sports section, was tucked under his arm. As he sat, his mother rushed in clipping an earring on, the other held between her teeth.

"Make sure you clean up after yourself," she managed to say despite the jewellery in her mouth. It was a continuation of the lecture she had begun last night when he had finally made it home. He had decided to keep Meghan's diary a secret from her. Last night, alone in his room, he had quickly gone through it, looking for anything that might indicate where she was hiding. He had slipped the elastic bands off and a mess of paper had cascaded onto his bedspread. There were old movie tickets, folded up handbills announcing bands playing at local clubs, bits of song lyrics or poems handwritten on restaurant napkins and pieces of cardboard.

He had noticed that a few pages had been ripped out of the diary. The reason was not immediately apparent; he assumed the particular entries had upset her in some way. On one bit of paper he found two names and two numbers. Despite the late hour, he rang them; both were no longer in service.

"I don't want to come home to another bowl of congealed milk and cereal," his mother interrupted his thoughts. She poured herself a cup of coffee. "And you better be home tonight. If you go downtown again, I'll ground you for the rest of the year!" She finished inserting the other earring, grabbed her coffee mug, and rushed off to complete some other part of her morning ritual.

Kyle pretended to ignore her and began pouring the Corn Bran into his bowl. As he did, he saw he was holding the French side toward him. *Son de Maïs*, it read. He remembered that's what Meghan used to call it.

"Hey, passe-moi the *Son de Maïs*!" she would call out. He smiled, remembering how much it bugged him back then, thinking she was showing off. She had often spoken in a confused version of English and French when she was trying to be funny. She had such a strange sense of humour compared to the rest of the family.

Kyle had spread the paper on the table in front of him, but had yet to start reading it. Instead, he thought about the entries in his sister's diary. He knew he hadn't been an ideal big brother, but it still hurt to realize just how badly he had treated Meghan.

"Must be nice," his mother said, rushing into the kitchen once more. "I wish I could just sit around reading the paper." She had said it half-jokingly — Kyle had picked up the tone. But he wasn't in the mood for her little jabs.

"Would you give me a break?" Kyle snapped back. He flipped the pages of the paper, still not able to concentrate, but refusing to look up at his mother. It amazed him how easily she could get under his skin. He shoved the cold cereal in his mouth, barely tasting it.

"I'm the one who could use the break!"

She stood over him now. She had been brushing her hair back, and the left side stood straight up. Her hair looked dry and coarse to Kyle, probably from too much hairspray and years of dyeing it to a shade much lighter than its natural one. For the first time in a long while, Kyle really looked at his mother. She seemed to have aged in some way, and she seemed wearier than he had ever seen her before. As she spoke she waved her hairbrush in his face.

"You have no idea what it's like for me, do you?" she said, her voice taking on that cold, calm tone Kyle always dreaded hearing. "I have to put that food on the table. I have to make sure we have a place to live."

"Yeah, I've heard it all before!" Kyle said. "But you're the one who let Dad walk all over you." Kyle immediately regretted saying it. They weren't even his own words. He had read them last night in Meghan's diary. He tried to cover, about to take another spoonful of cereal. His mother dropped her

20

brush and pulled the plate from the table and tossed it into the sink. It shattered, sending milk, cereal and bits of ceramic across the counter. He looked up at her, startled.

"Good. I have your full attention now, don't I?" She looked down at him, glaring. He couldn't look at her. "Don't you ever say that again. You have no idea what happened between your father and me. And until you've been in the same position, don't try to judge me!"

Kyle said nothing. He stared down at the table, at the paper he had lost interest in.

"I'm all you have right now! You better start listening to me!"

"Yeah. You're right. You are all I have right now. You made sure that Meghan didn't hang around!"

Then, unexpectedly, his mother burst into tears. Covering her face in her hands she rushed down the hall into the bathroom, slamming the door behind her. Kyle stood up and pushed the table away from him. His anger had begun to subside and he found he was stunned by his words, and his mother's reaction. He had expected anger, insults — anything but tears. In all of his life he could remember only a few times when his mother had broken down. Even after all that had happened between her and his father, not once had he seen her cry.

He walked carefully down the hall to the bath-room. The door never closed properly, unless you managed to line up the lock with the notch in the frame. It stood slightly ajar now. He could see his mother's back reflected in the mirror through the narrow opening. Her body shook with the force of her sobs. He felt helpless and terribly guilty. They had bickered forever it seemed, but not with this intensity. He realized as soon as he had said it that mentioning Meghan was a low blow. It seemed that these days the only words they exchanged were angry ones.

"Mom?" he said softly to her reflection. There was no response.

"Mom, look…" he began again.

"Just leave," was all she said.

Once again, he felt the blood rush to his cheeks, felt angry at himself for showing any weakness to her. He turned and headed for the door.

"Kyle, wait," he heard her say behind him. He ignored her. "Please, Kyle." Something in her voice made him stop and turn around. He felt his cheeks still burn and knew she must see his anger. Her eyes were red and puffy and she seemed so frail.

"We can't keep doing this," she said at last.

Kyle nodded. He could think of nothing more to say. He turned and continued on down the hall, stopping at the door to pick up his jacket and gym bag. He left, closing the door softly behind him.

\*\*\*

"And … ! Go!"

Kyle pushed off from a crouch and ran headlong at the bag. He felt a satisfying crunch as his shoulder pads hit the bag, heard the metal frame groan as the impact sent it backwards. It felt good to hit something that hard, even if it was just a practice bag. He looked to the west and saw the bowed arch of the chinook clouds. It was his first experience of a chinook and he liked it. The warm winds had brought the temperature up to nearly 18 degrees! A few leaves still clung to the trees at the far end of the football field, shaking in the mild breeze.

"Okay, Perry," Coach Kovacks said. "Stop beating up the equipment." He turned to the other boys lined up in squads waiting for their turn to hit the practice bags. "Come on, Curtis, move!"

Kyle ran out of the way, adjusting his equipment, pushing his helmet back to brush the sweat from his brow.

"Save some of that energy for the game tonight," Kovacks said to Kyle, grinning over at him. The coach was a short, stocky man in his mid-fifties. He was mostly bald with a fringe of thick, wiry hair that reminded Kyle of one of the Three Stooges, the one whose name he could never remember. Today the hair was tucked under a knit watch cap the same bottle green colour as the school sweatshirt the coach wore.

"Okay, team, listen up!" Kovacks shouted, then blew his whistle in two short bursts. It was the signal for everyone to huddle around him. "Let's go over our plan for tonight's game."

The boys all crouched around their coach as he began to speak. He started with the halfbacks, and in particular Kyle and Paul Christiansen. Paul had been the most promising player on the squad before Kyle had arrived. In only a few short months, Kyle had replaced Paul both on the team and off. Kyle's easy style, not to mention his looks, had helped him make friends quickly. Unlike his sister, he had no qualms about being the new kid in school. He had blended in immediately and hadn't expected it to be any other way. That process had made an enemy of Paul, though.

As the coach went over the game plan Kyle nodded, listening and at the same time trying to suppress a yawn.

"Keeping you awake, Perry?" the coach asked. Kyle had already seen that very little escaped the coach's eye.

"Sorry, coach," Kyle replied. "Late night."

"What's up?" Paul said, grinning. "Little sister not come home again last night?"

"Can it, Christiansen!" Kovacks shouted. Kyle glanced at Paul, then looked away. He was tired of his little remarks. Any chance he had to get a dig in, he'd take it, and had done so almost since the day Kyle had joined the team. Kyle had enough on his mind — he didn't need Paul's taunting as well. Fortunately, Paul decided to listen to the coach this time.

"Okay!" Kovacks said standing up to his full height, the teens all towering over him. He had quickly run through his plans for the first part of the game. "That's the strategy part over. Let's see if we can actually carry it off. Move!" He blew his whistle again and the team broke off into squads, one offence, the other defence. Paul Christiansen was in Kyle's squad and as they huddled together, Kyle saw Paul grin and glance around at the others.

"Hey, I got an idea how we can find Perry's sister!"

"The coach told you to drop it," Brian Hanlin, the quarterback, said.

"No, this is good! Why don't we take up a collection? We can take all the money down to the 10th Street stroll. I'm sure we won't have any trouble picking her up there, as long as we've got enough cash!"

Kyle moved with the speed and accuracy that had made him a place on the team. He hit Paul as hard as he had hit the practice bag, sending him sprawling on the grass. Within seconds, both boys had their helmets off, pounding their fists wherever they could find a vulnerable spot. Kyle had several inches and at least fifteen pounds on his opponent, but Paul was a more experienced fighter. Neither of them heard the whistle or the coach's shouts until hands were grabbing them, pulling them apart.

"What the hell is going on here?" Kovacks shouted. He looked quickly back and forth at the two boys, furious. Kyle and Paul only stared at each other, trying to catch their breath. Kyle felt a numbness over his left eye and blinked to keep blood from running into it. Both arms were pinned to his side by his teammates.

"Both of you off my field, now!" Kovacks shouted. "And I'll see you after practice. Separately!" he nodded to the others holding the boys. "Escort them back. And make sure they don't try to drown each other in the showers." With that he waved a dismissal and walked away, yelling at the others to get moving again.

***

"What's going on in your head, Perry?" Kovacks asked, leaning back in his chair, staring at Kyle huddled in his own wooden chair on the other side of the desk. The coach held a worn baseball, which he turned around and around in his left hand. Kyle stared at the ball, watching it spin hypnotically. The coach had the dexterity of a magician.

"You're a great kid. Popular, good looking. Smart enough, I guess," Kovacks said, the ball spinning around and around. "You're a good athlete, maybe even better than that. You have the potential of making a living at it. That's not something I see every day in this school. You following me?"

Kyle only nodded. He watched the ball spin around until it blocked out everything else but the sound of his coach's voice.

"You have all this anger inside you. You don't seem to be able to channel it."

"I didn't start it, Coach," Kyle said.

"I didn't ask who started it. I don't care who started it. All I care about is having to witness two of my best players, two seventeen-year-old kids trying to beat each other's skulls in." Kovacks paused and continued, "It's not the kind of thing that looks good on my record with the school board." Kyle glanced away from the spinning ball to his coach. There was a hint of a smile there.

26

"Look," he said, leaning forward and placing the ball on his weathered desk. "I can only guess at the kind of hell your life must be right now. But there are people here to help you. That's what the tax-payers pay them for."

Kyle nodded and wished he could stare at the spinning ball again. It was a distraction and he needed distractions.

"If you want, you can talk with me. Anytime," Kovacks said gently. "I may not have any answers, but I'll listen. How many players get that kind of offer from a coach?"

"I'm okay," Kyle said. "I can handle this."

Kovacks frowned at him. "Sure."

He sat up in his chair and pulled a folder from a pile of papers and charts. "I guess we both better get ready for the game."

Kyle looked at him, not believing what he had heard. He had expected to be suspended for the week, for tonight's game at the very least. Not knowing what to say, he stood, hoping to leave before Kovacks changed his mind.

"One more thing, Perry," Kovacks said as Kyle opened the office door. "One more situation like today and you're off my team. Permanently."

Kyle only nodded and left, closing the door gently behind him.

# Chapter 4

September 5

Dear Me,

So, my first day at school was just as wonderful as I thought it would be. Good old Dad would have called it a "self-fulfilling prophecy." He'd say that I went to school expecting it to be a lousy experience and therefore it turned out to be one. He'd never consider for a second that just maybe I was right.

Maybe it wasn't as bad as I thought as far as the hick stuff goes. There were some girls that looked okay, a couple of cute guys — although none in my class of course! I guess guys are the same everywhere, the cool ones, the tough ones, the geeks, and the jocks.

Big Brother will love it. The first thing I saw was a huge banner over the front entrance welcoming back the "Marlborough Monarchs — Foothills' Champions!" Champions of what I didn't ask. If they're like Big Brother and his pals back home, they'll be champions of bad haircuts, bad attitudes and, of course, bad smells!

I didn't see one cowboy hat, but there were plenty of cowboy boots. Both girls and boys wore them. There were even girls wearing them with short, frilly jean skirts. I thought that went out with the eighties! I guess most kids didn't look that much different than kids back in good old Thornhill. Poorer, maybe.

I know, I know … I sound like such a snob again, but I can't help myself. They all looked so tough! Especially the girls!

Thank God I didn't wear anything too nice. I think some of the rougher girls would've beaten me up over it. Or tried. I think I could stand up for myself. And besides, if they did do something, I'd get them back. There were a couple of kids in my class who looked okay, but mostly everyone kept to their own groups. My homeroom teacher, Mrs. Chubbie (yes, that is her real name!!), had to embarrass me by introducing me to the class, telling them where I came from and stuff. As if I didn't already feel like a mutant! She's not going to be fun, I can tell (from my vast experience with homeroom teachers.) She's one of those teachers who loves the sound of her own voice, pronounces every word perfectly. She let it be known right away that it's a privilege to be taught by someone of her obviously superior intelligence and skills.

I nearly forgot! There's this other girl in my class. She looks really, really weird. But kind of cool, too. I really wanted to talk to her, especially after what she did during attendance. Mrs. Chubbie wrote her name on the board and made a point of telling everyone the proper way to pronounce it.

"Now class," she said, "my name is Mrs. Chubbie. I know how most of you would like to pronounce it, but the correct pronunciation is Mrs. Shew-bay."

She pronounced it a couple of times. Shew-bay, Sheew-bay, Sheeew-bay! I was already trying not to laugh out loud at this, and then guess what? She made us all say it in unison! Imagine a classroom full of grade 9s all saying Shew-bay, Shew-bay, out loud, over and over.

This woman is seriously disturbed! And of course, she is more than a little Shew-bay! She's pretty much Ohhh-beeece!

So then, later, she starts taking attendance. Everything's going along pretty well until she gets to this gothic-looking girl. You know, all pale and wearing black. Even her hair was black. She wore one of those Egyptian crosses on this thick bike chain around her neck.

"Janice Morgan?" Mrs. Shew-bay calls out. There's no answer. Mrs. Shew-bay looks up, confused. She looks at the goth-girl, like she knew all along who she was.

"Janice?" she asks again, a little miffed now. There's a little more silence, then we hear a voice from way in the back.

"It's Jan-eece," the goth-girl says.

"Pardon me?" Mrs. Shew-bay asks very properly.

"My name is pronounced Jan-eece. Not Janice."
The whole class tries to stop from laughing out
loud at this. All eyes were now looking at the girl
slouched in the back row.

"I see," Mrs Shew-bay says, taking off her glasses
and looking mighty disturbed. It's pretty obvious
to everyone, even the beauty queens in the centre
aisle, that this goth-girl is making fun of the teacher's
little pronunciation lecture.

"Well, Miss Morgan," Mrs. Shew-bay goes on,
her own pronunciation still perfect. "I believe you
were in my class for a brief time last year. Unless
I'm mistaken, during your short stay, you answered
to the name Janice."

"I've changed since last year. Janice is the name
of some average, boring student. Do I look average
to you?"

Mrs. Shew-bay was getting even more red in the
face. She didn't like this kind of attitude from one
of her students.

"I'm afraid I gave up trying to know what students think when they look at themselves in the
mirror. However, there is one thing that's very
average about you, Miss Morgan." She paused for
effect, then looked up: "Your grades."

Janeece laughed out loud! I couldn't believe it.
How cool can you get? Laughing when a teacher
slams you in front of everybody!

I guess we all figured it was a pretty good shot.
Old Mrs. Shew-bay could dish it out as well. When
the class had settled down once more, she looked
up at Janeece.

"Despite your need to stand out from the hoi polloi, Miss Morgan — "

(I had to look *hoi polloi* up. I couldn't believe it was an actual word.)

"In my class I will continue to refer to you as Janice."

"Whatever you say ... Mrs. Chubby," Janeece replied — straight-faced! The whole class broke up! Including me!

Old Mrs. Shew-bay went even more red. I thought she was going to pop an artery. But she managed to stay pretty calm and got us to calm down too before we left for first period. Still, Janeece sure got off on the wrong foot with Mrs. Shew-bay. I get the feeling she's the kind of teacher that holds a grudge.

Other than that, everything went pretty much as usual. At lunch I sat with two other girls from my class, both transferred from other schools this year. I guess we were the outcasts grouping together. One girl is Melissa, she moved here from Red Deer. She's kind of short and thin, with that awful wiry, red hair that always look fake. She's okay, I guess, a little timid for me. The other girl is Jennifer, she's from someplace in Saskatchewan. She's more like me, your run-of-the-mill, flat-chested, nondescript brunette type.

Of course, the only thing anyone wanted to talk about was Janeece and Mrs. Shew-bay! It was pretty cool, a great way to break the ice. Pretty soon everyone at the table was talking about it. Janeece was sitting way at the back of the lunchroom, reading a beat-up old book and drinking some blood red stuff. (Let's hope it was just tomato juice). She stayed away from the sun, preferring the shadows.

She really knew how to play up on her image, I'll give her that.

Melissa and Jennifer were okay, I guess. We're going to maybe do something this weekend, go downtown or something. I'd really like to talk to Janeece, though. She looks like she might be interesting to get to know.

That's about it for now. Until next time …

— Meghan

# Chapter 5

Kyle paced back and forth outside the classroom, tossing a baseball up in the air. He had tried spinning it around just as he had seen Coach Kovacks do, but today his fingers seemed too large and clumsy for such a delicate task. He kept trying, though.

This morning, before going to school, he had taken Meghan's photocopy of this semester's class schedule. If she had still been there, her chemistry class would be getting out any second now. As he waited, he looked over the schedule. He smiled, thinking it was typical Meghan. The classes she liked — English, Biology, even Chemistry — had little red hearts drawn inside the schedule squares. Those classes she especially liked received double or even triple hearts. The classes she hated had a similar code, this time using tiny pitchforks. He felt an overwhelming moment of sadness, thinking of her scribbling away, just like any other fourteen year old. Kyle looked up at the clock and saw it was almost the end of the period. He folded the schedule and placed it in the pocket of his team jacket, then nervously rubbed his newly buzzed head. The bristly feel of his close-cropped hair was somehow comforting.

The bell rang loudly in the empty hall and almost immediately doors opened and students rushed out. The change in noise level was incredible. He kept dodging other kids, trying to keep his eye on the door of Meghan's chemistry class, looking for two girls in particular. He was beginning to think they had skipped class when he saw them emerge, books held tightly to their chests. They saw him as he made his way through the heavy sea of kids. As he got closer, he saw them exchange a nervous look.

"Hi," Kyle said, finally reaching them. The girls seemed to slouch against each other and he felt he was towering over them. "It's Melissa and Jennifer, right?"

"I didn't think you knew our names," the brunette, Jennifer, replied. Kyle remembered the brief description his sister had written in her diary of these girls. She was right about Melissa, a thin, pale girl with brassy red hair. Meghan thought she resembled Jennifer, but Kyle couldn't see it. They both had similar hair colour, but Meghan's was thick and healthy looking; Jennifer's just kind of hung limply. Meghan was never as outgoing as Kyle, but she had never cringed the way this girl seemed to.

"I guess you want to ask us about Meghan, right?" Jennifer asked. Her attitude and her manner seemed to exude defeat. He found it uncomfortable talking to people who appeared to think so little of themselves. Kyle remembered their reaction when they had first spotted him waiting outside their classroom. He knew that for a brief moment, they thought he was there just to see one of them, to maybe ask her out. He had seen girls react that way before. Kyle was reminded of entries in Meghan's diary. Was he acting like a snob now? If he was, he found he couldn't help himself. After all, first impressions were everything, right?

Up close like this, he saw they weren't unattractive, but there was nothing about them that would make you notice them. And their lack of self-esteem would have turned him off by now, even if he was interested in girls their age.

"The principal and the police have already asked us a million questions," Jennifer said. "Why would you think we'd know anything more?"

Kyle hadn't even had a chance to answer her first question. "I just thought you might be able to help me with something."

"It's been a long time, too, hasn't it?" Melissa piped up, finding her voice at last. "I mean since anyone heard from her, right?"

"About a month, I guess," Kyle replied.

"Everyone in class thinks that's she's probably ..."

"Melissa!" Jennifer rammed an elbow into her friend's side, shutting her up. The girl looked at her friend angrily then hung her head, her face turning red.

"She's so dense sometimes!" Jennifer said to Kyle.

"It's okay," Kyle said. "I know what every-one's saying."

"You know, we never really hung around much? With Meghan? We did a bit at first, but then …" her voice just faded off. Kyle found Jennifer's style of speech grating. Every statement sounded like a question.

"Meghan wanted to hang out with the cool kids, so she kind of dumped us," Melissa interjected. "'Course, that didn't work out either. Probably 'cause she hung out with us. And because of where you live and stuff."

"Melissa!" Jennifer shouted again, rolling her eyes at Kyle. He nodded. He was well aware of the opinion most people had of his neighbourhood.

"There was a girl in your class, used to be a street kid. Meghan mentioned her. She had dyed black hair, dressed kind of weird …"

"Janice!" Melissa replied.

"Jan-eece," Jennifer corrected her. "She really *was* weird."

"Has she been in class lately?"

"Janeece?" Jennifer said. "No way. She dropped out about the end of September. Mrs. Chubbie gave her a hard time. So did most of the other teachers. But I don't blame them, she was really strange."

"You know where I can find her?"

Both girls looked at each other and shrugged.

"She said her last name was Morgan, but I don't think it was her real last name," Jennifer said. "She was a foster kid or something. Thought she was too cool, taking off all the time, living on the street …"

She stopped and looked embarrassed again, as if realizing she had dissed a fellow classmate.

"I don't suppose you know where she was living?"

The girls look at each other. "Well," Melissa said, "we're not weird or anything. You won't tell anyone, will you?"

Kyle shook his head, annoyed and puzzled by the conversation. He was having a hard time keeping track of the convoluted way of speaking these girls had. He had the urge to grab and shake them until they made sense.

"One day, the three of us? You know, us two and Meghan?" Jennifer began.

"It was Meghan's idea. She was totally fascinated by Janeece," Melissa added.

Kyle nodded, then stared at Jennifer, willing her to continue, even though he wanted this entire episode to end. "Anyway," Jennifer said. "We kind of followed her home after school one day?"

"She didn't see you?" Kyle asked.

"No," Melissa said. "She was reading. She always had her nose stuck in some book. Not school books, either. Her own stuff." Kyle remembered Meghan was always reading books not on the school list. She actually read because she enjoyed it. He felt a momentary twinge of guilt remembering the times he had harassed her about it.

"She lived in this really horrible complex," Jennifer continued. "It looked like it was full of druggies and bikers and stuff."

"It was pretty scary," Melissa added.

"You remember which one?" Kyle pressed.

"We don't know the area that well either," Jennifer said.

"Did Meghan tell you we just moved here too?" Melissa asked.

Kyle nodded, impatient to get away.

"I guess I could show it to you," Jennifer added.

"That's okay," Kyle said quickly. He couldn't stand the thought of continuing this conversation any longer than he had to. "If you could just give me directions."

"It's no trouble, we'd like too," Jennifer said.

Kyle kept talking, explaining that he had to go this morning, right away, that they still had classes. It took several more minutes, but he finally convinced them to draw him a map. He thanked them again and began to walk away quickly.

"Kyle," he heard Jennifer call out beside him. He kept walking, just turning to glance at her as she tried to keep up his pace.

"I just wanted to say that, you know ..."

"What?" he said curtly.

"I just wanted to say that if you needed someone to talk to ... you could call me or something." She blushed. "I mean call *us*."

Maybe he was being too harsh, just like he had always been with Meghan. He forced himself to slow down and look at her.

"Thanks. Maybe I will." He and Jennifer made eye contact for a split second before she broke it off, looking down at her feet.

"Thanks again, for everything," he said before walking away once more.

Kyle looked over the townhouses that formed a semicircle in the cul-de-sac. He guessed that originally the stucco had been painted a pale beige, with a natural wood trim. Now the colour had faded and the stucco itself had broken away in places, rusted mesh showing through. The wood trim had faded and warped through years of neglect.

The street out front was littered with garbage and discarded vehicles. An old El Camino lay rusting in a front yard, two wheels gone, the naked axle resting on cracked cinderblocks. One of the houses had half a dozen orange leaf bags with jack-o'-lantern faces printed on them. Stray animals or kids had ripped into them, strewing their contents across the front lawn. He smiled at the thought of anyone referring to the patch of brown grass and cracked cement out front as a lawn. None of the orange bags contained leaves.

He saw the house the girls had described. Three boys ran about screaming, all of them underdressed, for a chilly November day like this. They ignored him as he walked up to the house, the one with the neon green storm door slightly ajar over the concrete steps. As he walked up he saw that the house was slightly better kept than those surrounding it. The tiny lawn was clear of litter and the tiny shrubs growing near the steps were covered in canvas and string for the winter. Standing at the door, he saw the kids now paid more attention to him. Kyle looked once more at the three boys dressed in faded T-shirts and clear plastic sandals.

He rang the doorbell twice and could clearly hear it buzz inside. He waited a few moments and when nothing happened, he opened the screen door and knocked. As he did, the front door slid ajar slightly. Again there was no reply, but now he could hear movement inside, and the low murmur of a television. Kyle knocked again, louder this time. The door opened even wider and he saw a bare entranceway, stairs to his right leading up.

"Whaddaya want?" a woman's voice shouted from upstairs.

Kyle felt a little foolish yelling through a partly closed door. He knocked again. This time he heard a muffled voice — a man's. He heard the woman laugh.

"Whatever you're selling, we don't want it!" the man shouted from upstairs.

"I'm not selling anything!" Kyle replied at last. "I'm looking for someone!"

He turned to see that the kids had stopped playing altogether and were staring at him. There was something about their eyes he found disturbing. There was no more response from inside, but the volume on the TV went up dramatically. He began pounding on the door now, really putting his arm behind it. For a second he thought that these people, no matter how they lived, had the right not to respond to some stranger at their door. Then he decided that his search was more important than the minor inconvenience he was causing them.

A door opened somewhere upstairs, and he heard muffled swearing and footsteps running down the stairs. Kyle looked up as a girl ran down, tying a faded robe around her thin body. Kyle was shocked to see that she was about his age.

"What the hell d'you want?" the girl demanded. She was small, barely over five feet, but she had a presence that made Kyle take a step back from her. Her hair was long, dyed a horrible shade of orange and was sticking up at the back. Her feet were bare and her toes were painted a green similar to the screen door. Even though her hands were empty, she reeked of cigarette smoke.

"I'm looking for Janice," he said. He pronounced it Janeece, like Jennifer had.

"Janeece?" the girl asked, her voice still jarringly loud. "You talking about Janice?"

Before he could reply, the girl looked down past him. "What the hell you staring at? You wanted to play out here! So go play!"

"We're cold, Cathy!" one of the boys replied. The three of them had gathered around the bottom step, and Kyle realised they had been staring at him because they lived here. He saw nothing in their features that made him think they were related to each other, or to this girl.

"So what? I'm not your mother!" she shouted.

"We're telling Mrs. Reed!" This was from the tallest of the boys. The girl in the robe flushed, glaring at him. "All right," she said at last. "But I don't want any of you sneaking upstairs. And you better not tell June about me having Mike over, either."

The boys screamed and shouted promises as they ran inside. Cathy moved aside as they charged down the hall. In the silence that followed, she looked back up at Kyle. "You don't look like her type," she said, continuing the conversation where she had left it.

"She knew my sister," Kyle said. "I wanted to see if she could help me find her."

"Maybe," the girl said. "I guess you'd have to find Janice first, wouldn't you?"

"She's not here?"

"You kidding?" Cathy said. "First chance she got, boom, she hit the streets again! You know how long it took June to get the paperwork done on her? Man, she was pissed!"

"Is June the foster mother?"

Cathy just looked at him as if he were stupid.

"Could I talk to her?"

"She's shopping. Buying more lousy junk for dinner."

"Do you know where Janice stays when she's on the street?" he asked. Before she could reply, the man upstairs shouted down. From the voice, Kyle could tell the man was much older than Cathy.

"I'm coming!" Cathy shouted. With that, she stepped back and slammed the door in Kyle's face. Angry, he turned away, shoving his hands in his pockets and jogging down the steps.

He sucked in a gulp of cold November air, wishing for another Chinook, and walked quickly away, wanting to get free of this place as quickly as possible.

# Chapter 6

October 3
Dear Me,
Wow!

I was just looking at my entries and it looks like I've been neglecting the ol' diary for a while. This is my first entry in nearly two weeks. But what a cool two weeks it's been!

School still isn't much better. I was totally bored hanging out with Melissa and Jennifer after about a week. All the other girls thought they were too cool to bother with me. Well, maybe I didn't give them much of a chance. I was really hoping to get to know Janice. I've never actually seen a goth-girl up close like that before. Everyone said she was weird and lived on the streets and did all kinds of stuff. I don't know why, but it made me want to get to know her even more.

I tried to talk to her a couple of times, but she pretty much ignored me. The last time, I tried to talk to her about this movie I had seen once, about kids living on the street.

She stopped me right away.

"Why are you telling me this?" she asked. Kind of nasty, I thought. I said I was just trying to make conversation. She just grabbed her books and stood up and said something about living on the streets not being a movie. Then she walked off and I could see everyone stare at me. It was completely embarrassing! After that, I kind of acted like her. Just kept to myself. Who needs girlfriends anyway?

Okay! So I've waited long enough to tell you the really great news — I met someone! His name is Stephen and he's about the coolest guy I've ever seen. And guess what? We're going steady! For nearly two whole weeks now!

So, in case I forget when I'm forty and my memory isn't what it used to be, let me describe the man of my dreams! First of all, he really is a man, not just some zit-faced kid. He's 17, he'll be 18 this weekend! He's really tall and has gorgeous blue, blue eyes and dark, wavy hair and he has this cool tattoo on his right arm, like a ring of thorns going all the way around (he works out, so the arm looks pretty cool too).

So does the rest of him!

He's super nice, too. Especially to me. And not like all wimpy kind of nice, like some boys who are so nice they make you kind of sick, you know? Like you lose all respect for them? He's nice, but he still has a mind of his own and he doesn't let me walk all over him.

So how did all this happen? Well, that's pretty cool too.

Big Brother finally granted me the privilege of going downtown with him two Saturdays ago. We went to Stephen Avenue Mall, which is this long street only for people. They don't let cars on it. The inside mall part is really only a bunch of buildings all hooked up with walkways. Supposedly you can go all through downtown without ever going outside. Unlike the underground concourses back in old T.O., you can actually see daylight when you walk around.

Big Brother got hungry after about 15 minutes so we had to go to the food court near Eaton's. Of course, he meets a bunch of his football pals, all dressed up in their team jackets and wearing the same brushcut they think is so jock!

And, of course, now Kyle is embarrassed to be seen with his little sister so he tells me to go get something to eat. So off I go to sit in a corner alone with bad Chinese food while watching all these people have fun. While I'm eating and trying not to look like a total loser, I see this guy sitting all alone as well, drinking a Coke and not looking at all bothered that he's by himself. Then these two really tough-looking girls bump into me.

"You finished?" one of them says to me.

"I just sat down," I reply.

"You think you're special or something?" the other one says. I don't want to make eye contact with them so I just try to keep on eating. I look around for Big Brother, but he's way on the other side of the food court, acting cool.

"You got a whole table to yourself!" the first one says. "And here's two of us still waiting for one."

"I guess I got lucky," I say, trying to sound casual and not provoke them in any way.

"You better eat someplace else if you want to stay lucky," the other one says. I look up at her for the first time and I see that neither of them have any food.

"What's up?" a guy asks. I look away from the two tough girls and the guy who was sitting alone has walked over to my table.

"What's it to you?" the first tough girl asks.

"It looks like you're bothering my friend here."

The two girls look at each other. This guy looks like someone they don't want to tangle with. But they don't want to just walk away.

"Why don't you take my table?" he says, nodding to the one he just left.

"If you know each other, how come you weren't sitting together?" the first girl asks.

The guy smiles and looks at me. "I was waiting for her to invite me."

I look up at him, then at the two girls and back at him. He seems to be waiting for something. Then it clicks! I can be so dense sometimes!

"Oh! Oh yeah!" I say, finally catching on. "Sure. Sit down." (Or something like that. It was probably even dumber!)

He sits down and the girls give us one last look and go sit at the other table.

"You okay?" he asks.

"Sure," I say. I try to take a casual sip of my drink but my hand is shaking. "That was pretty intense. Thanks."

He just shrugs and grins. "No problem. They were just big talkers."

He waits, like he expects me to say something, but I can't even think. All the noise and crowd and those two girls wanting to beat me up and now this gorgeous guy is sitting at my table waiting for me to start a conversation. Not to mention what all of this and the fried rice was doing to my stomach!

"I'm Stephen," he says.

"Pardon me?" I reply. I was so busy thinking of something to say that I wasn't paying attention.

"Stephen. You know? Like in the mall?"

I must have looked really confused.

"Sorry, bad joke." Of course I still had no idea what he was talking about. Then I remembered. We were in the Stephen Avenue Mall.

"My first time," I say.

"What?" he says. Great, I think. Now I'm confusing both of us!

"My first time at the mall here," I say, trying to explain.

"Really? You're not from Calgary?"

So, then I explain where I came from and all that, hoping I'm not boring him. He tells me that he had seen me when I first came in, that he had sat near me deliberately.

"I guess it was your hair," he said.

"My hair?"

"Yeah. It was the first thing I noticed. It's gorgeous."

"No it isn't," I said. "It's a mess!" He said that girls pay a fortune getting perms and stuff to get their hair to look the way my hair does naturally. I was going to ask him how he knew mine was natural, but I figured I'd let him talk.

We sat there for about half an hour, I guess, talking. Then he asked me if I wanted to go for a walk. I wasn't sure at first. Here I was with this total stranger, so much older than me! Then I saw big brother laughing with his pals, checking out the girls. I thought he'd have a stroke when he finally remembered me and then saw I had gone. Besides, Stephen was really nice and I'm a pretty good judge of people. I knew I'd be safe with him.

So, I left Big Brother behind and went for a walk with Stephen!

We walked for hours and just talked. He didn't try anything, and maybe I wouldn't have minded if he did. When it started to get cold outside, he took me to this indoor garden. It was incredible, like something out of a science fiction movie. It was different levels of trees and streams and fish and birds, all glassed in! All around outside you could see office buildings and traffic, but we were all warm and cosy inside this park. Maybe by the time I'm my dad's age, this is how we'll all be living. Under glass.

He bought us drinks and we sat in this secluded bench way up over the rest of the gardens. The only bad thing was seeing all these kids my age or younger just hanging out there. They looked hungry and filthy.

Stephen told me they were street kids, this was one of the places they hung out to get warm. They look kind of scary, but kind of pathetic as well.

"They are kind of pathetic," Stephen said when I told him what I was thinking. "That's why I got off the street."

"You were a street kid?" I asked him.

"Sure. I was on the street when I was nine."

"Nine?" I say. It sounds so horrible. A nine-year-old living on the streets by himself. Although, not exactly by himself. Stephen says most kids form a kind of street family, with the older kids looking out for the younger ones.

"It's still pretty pathetic," he said. "That's why I got out of it. Got a job and a place to live."

He didn't tell me a lot about his life, or how he managed to get off the streets. I just thought he was even more amazing for doing all that stuff.

Stephen has a job as a courier and he really does have his own place! Which I've seen (but more about that later!)

So! I finally got home that night about eight. And, of course, all hell broke loose!

Big Brother was sitting on the couch and just glared at me as I walked in. There was no TV on or anything, just silence. I tried to sneak down the hall to my room, but in this place, a roach couldn't sneak anywhere without being seen.

"Meghan!" my mother screams at me. "Where have you been?" She tells me we were supposed to go to Grandma's for dinner and that she had to make up some excuse so she didn't have to tell her

50

mother that I was wandering the streets all day. What's the big deal about telling her? It's not like I'm eight or something.

Mom goes on and on for like half an hour about how worried she was, how she was ready to call the police and on and on. I just let her rant for a while, hoping she'd get over it but she kept on going!

"As if you're really worried about me!" I shout back at last, fed up. "All you've ever worried about is yourself." That really sets her off!

She goes on about how all she ever does is try to provide for us, to watch out for us and the usual garbage. So I say that back home all she ever did was go to the club and play tennis and join her little committees or take courses she never used and act like the big shot rich wife. She sent us off to school and had people clean the house and didn't know or care where I was half the time. I told her I was always hanging out downtown but back then, the house was big enough that I could get away with it and I just had to see her when absolutely necessary! I was getting her pretty good! I could tell by the look on her face. She wasn't just acting, she was really hurt by all this.

Kyle tried to get us to shut up, said something about the neighbours hearing us three houses away. Mom and I ignored him, we were pretty deep into it. And it had been building for a while.

Okay! In my diary, knowing only I will ever read these pages, I will admit that I felt a little guilty while I was arguing with her. Part of me knew I was wrong in staying out and that I had probably really scared her. But part of me wanted to keep on getting her for turning my whole life upside down. Besides, it was like we were running downhill, you know? Once you get going, you keep going faster and faster and the only way you can stop is letting yourself fall (or maybe hit a tree). I wasn't going to fall down for her anymore!

Big Brother left, all disgusted with us, after trying to get us to stop. He doesn't like this kind of behaviour, it embarrasses him when we act like emotional women or something. He's just like good old Pop!

"Why should I listen to you?" I shouted. "You can't even take care of your own life. Why would I let you run mine?"

"I'm still your mother!" she says. I nearly laughed at that one.

"You're still pathetic!" I reply. "Look at us now! You let Dad walk all over you! All over us! He got everything and we end up in this lousy place with no friends, no nothing!"

"You don't know what happened!" she screams. "You have no idea what happened between your father and me!"

"Sure I do! He knew he could walk all over you! He knew you'd just cave in and let him! Just like you always do!"

"He humiliated me!" she screamed back. "I couldn't stay there, with everyone laughing behind my back. And all the people I thought were my friends just dropped me. They put up with me because of who I was married to, not because of me!"

Then she put her hand over her mouth and turned away, like she had said more than she wanted to. This really got to me, even as angry as I was. I guess I hadn't really thought about it from her side that much. We kept on shouting stuff for a bit longer, but it was pretty much over. I ran to my room and slammed the door. I felt bad about the fight and about what I said. But I wanted to live my own life too. Thinking about the day I'd had with Stephen helped me feel better. Sure she was hurt, but she chose her life! I was born into it, I didn't have any choice.

But now I do. And I want to keep seeing Stephen.

It's been pretty tense around here when Mom and I are in the same room. Fortunately, because of her hours, it doesn't happen a lot. Big Brother was grounded for a week, and I was grounded for two. Of course, as soon as she's gone I sneak out. I've seen Stephen almost every day since we met. I've even skipped school to meet him. He took time off of his job — he says his boss is pretty cool that way. We went to his place on Monday. It's kind of small and dirty, but it's all his. He doesn't have to share it with anyone. Unless he wanted to.

So far, he's still been pretty good. We kiss and stuff but he doesn't make me do anything I don't want to. He knows I'm a little scared. It's not like I've had tons of experience with boys his age. I just hope he keeps being patient with me — I don't want to lose him.

Oh yeah, something strange happened on Monday, before we went to his place. We were at the gardens. (I asked him to take me there again, it's so warm and beautiful.) When he left to get us a drink, I saw Janeece with a couple of other kids. They were all pretty much ultra-goth. I waved at her, hoping she would remember me from school. She only lasted there about a month, then she disappeared. She had noticed me and Stephen, but just ignored me pretty much.

So I was sitting alone, just staring at the stream and the fish when I heard this voice behind me. I jumped and looked around. It was Janice. I was shocked that she could sneak up on me, past these narrow benches, without my hearing her. Maybe she really is a vampire.

She was still all in black, like at school, and her face was as white as a sheet and she wore this blood red lipstick. A little girl was beside her, just staring up at me. She looked like a miniature copy of Janice. She had this weird thing on her lip, like a big red birthmark or something.

"Hi," I manage to say. "I haven't seen you in class for a while." Lame, but I had to say something.

"You know anything about that guy you're with?" she said. She didn't respond to what I said at all. Just stared at me with this blank expression. So did the girl. Very spooky, especially with Halloween so close.

"He's my boyfriend," I said. She didn't react to that, just looked over at him, waiting in line at the snack counter.

"You know him?" I asked. She was making me a little nervous. Maybe she was weirder than she

54

looked. I was beginning to regret wanting her to notice me.

"I know who he works for," she said. "Maybe you should find your boyfriends at school."

"Maybe I'll do what I want," I replied, getting a little ticked. Who did she think she was? And besides, what was she telling me? I should worry about Stephen's boss?

Janice looked me up and down, then was about to say something else. The little girl tugged at her sleeve and she looked down at her. The little girl was looking past her, at the snack bar. Janice and I both looked over and saw that Stephen was coming back with drinks. When I looked back again, Janice and the girl were gone.

"What did they want?" Stephen asked when he sat down beside me.

"Money," I said. "I told them to get lost." I'm not sure why I lied to him.

"Good for you!" Stephen said. "I hate being panhandled by these kids!"

I was about to remind him that he was once just like them, but decided to keep quiet once more.

Other than that weird little incident, things have been pretty great in my life. It's Stephen's birthday this weekend and there's a big party at his place. I can't wait! Who knows? Maybe I might just spend the whole weekend there, if he wants me to. Stay tuned …

— Meg

# Chapter 7

Kyle took a sip of his drink, finishing it off with a final slurp that tasted of cold, watery syrup.

He stood up and threw the container in the trash can beside the bench. The bench was hard and worn — made of logs in an attempt to look rustic. The air inside was moist; it smelled strange and not entirely pleasant. If he tried hard enough, Kyle could see the appeal the Devonian Gardens would have had for his sister. It did seem like a set in a science fiction movie, all these trees and birds kept under glass. It was snowing outside and he watched the flakes fall gently on the streets below. It was a little disorienting, seeing winter on the other side of glass while he stood in shirt sleeves in the moist air of a tropical forest.

Looking a little closer, he thought it was seedier than Meghan had described in her diary. The ashtrays were full, and men and women in business clothes ate hurriedly and self-consciously from paper bags or trays from the food court. A shallow stream wandered aimlessly throughout the garden, stocked with huge, bloated fish. They swarmed together, lifting their mouths hungrily out of the dank water, hoping some friendly passer-by would toss them food sold from nearby dispensers. Statues of children frolicking and baby deer stopping for a drink hid among the thick ferns and the broad, rubbery leaves of plants. There were little signs identifying the plants and the person or organization that had donated them.

Kyle wandered along, pushing past a throng of middle-aged tourists, clustered together to take a group picture. He climbed up to the highest part of the gardens, and as he sat he looked down to see layers and layers of plants and benches, terraced below him. Closing his eyes, Kyle could hear the relaxing sound of falling water and birdsong. Maybe, he thought, if he was in love with a girl and here with her, he might have described this place the way Meghan had.

Kyle wondered if he had ever felt about any girl the way Meghan felt about this Stephen. He smiled and shook his head. What was going on here? Why was he having all these crazy thoughts? It had to be Meghan and her diary! Just because she had to analyse every thought, every feeling, did that mean he had to as well? He decided, only half-jokingly, that reading her diary was a bad influence on him.

Here he was, skipping class, hanging out downtown, wasting time. Just like Meghan. Bad enough, but now he was also getting thoughtful, starting to question himself. He should have asked Brian or

Ollie or some of the other guys to skip with him. At least with the guys around he didn't have the time to waste thinking about if he'd ever really been in love!

Something inside made him need to do this alone. He didn't know why, but searching for Meghan with the guys felt wrong. Kyle wasn't sure where this feeling came from. All his life he had been a team player, he'd never had a reason or the desire to do things by himself. Since he was being so analytical these days, he began to see that he had always needed to be with others, that it had been a little frightening to be alone. Only losers did stuff alone.

He wondered if things would be different now if he had spent more time with Meghan and less with his pals. Would it have been so difficult to spend the afternoon with her? He could have taken her here, rather then let her come with a guy who picked her up in a mall. He tried to remember a time when he and Meghan were close and found it difficult. They had always been so different. Before the divorce, before the move to Calgary, before the bitterness, he remembered a different girl. One who laughed easily, who liked to tease him endlessly about everything from his choice of clothes to his choice of girls. At the time her teasing had irritated him, often because he wouldn't quite get the joke. All his life he had been aware that Meghan was smarter than him, that she had a quick wit and a way of sizing people up. He prayed that sense was still with her. She'd need it now more than ever.

Kyle opened his eyes and looked down. Angry voices had snapped him away from his thoughts. About three or four levels below him, he saw two men, probably security, trying to clear some kids from the benches. The kids were swearing at them, not willing to move away without a show of protest. Finally, as he watched, the kids left, the guards sticking with them until the elevator doors closed. Kyle looked at his watch. He had been here for over two hours. He wondered how long before security came along to get rid of him. Can't have these teenagers hanging around, upsetting the office workers, he thought.

Kyle stood up and stretched, feeling his back ache from sitting too long on these uncomfortable benches. He slipped on his jacket and walked slowly over to the same elevator the kids had used.

***

"You want your bill now?"

Kyle looked up, startled. He had been lost in his own thoughts and hadn't heard the waitress walk over to him. He looked up at her, seeing the ring piercing her left nostril, the strange glow of her neon yellow hair.

"I guess …" Kyle said. He wasn't sure if he was finished or not. He wanted to keep warm, wait here a little longer before he went back out on the street again. It had been a week since he had found Meghan's diary. Every night he could sneak away, he was back downtown, asking questions. Trying

59

to find Janice. His instincts told him that she was the key to finding his sister.

"It isn't brain surgery," the waitress said.

"What?" Kyle asked.

"All I want to know is if you want your bill or not!"

The girl looked tired and bored. Kyle was a little annoyed at her attitude. Back home, he and his friends had loved giving waiters and waitresses a hard time. Complaining, sending things back, telling them they'd messed up orders, just goofing around. It had seemed like harmless fun back then. Kids their own age were treated the worst. Kyle had always felt embarrassed by being served by kids his age — it seemed wrong. He had wondered why they felt it necessary to go out and work for a few dollars a week. None of his circle had ever needed to. He fished in his pocket and pulled out his money, a fairly thick pile of bills. Barely looking at the amount, he tossed it on the tray. "Keep the change," he mumbled. The girl didn't respond. She just picked it up and turned to the next table.

Kyle yawned as he looked at his watch. It was a little past 10. His mother would be arriving home any minute now. He knew how she would react to find him out once more. He didn't care. She had very little control over his actions these days.

As he stood, he noticed a group of about three or four boys leaning against the far wall, talking amongst themselves, taking a new interest in him. Two of the boys looked vaguely familiar, especially the one with the green hair. He couldn't place them. After all, he had studied a sea of kids on these outings.

Kyle felt the cold air rush into his lungs as he stepped outside the Koop. It had stopped snowing hours ago, and he looked up to see a clear, star-filled sky. The night had turned bitterly cold now. He zipped up his jacket and readied himself for the long walk to the Drop-In Centre, the first place on his nightly rounds. He had begun to follow a cir-cuit, checking each of the places a street kid might stay at night. He knew that it was only a matter of time before he would run into Meghan in one of them. He heard the door of the coffee shop open behind him and stepped aside to let whoever was there out, not bothering to look back.

As the lights on 1st and 12th changed, Kyle sprinted across, feeling, as always, the rush of pride as his muscles reacted quickly and gracefully. It felt good to move again after so many hours of just sitting, watching. He was across the street in sec-onds, then across 12th against the lights, slowing on the other side, beside the grounds of the TransCal building. The area was dark, badly lit, and he knew it was a hangout for street kids. In the shadows they bought and sold drugs. Some wandered past him now, glassy eyed and oblivious to his presence.

A dog began to bark wildly, and Kyle glanced across the street to see a huge Doberman, stuck on a narrow balcony of the trendy condo there. He slowed his pace to watch it, strangely fascinated by the sight of the powerful dog pacing back and forth, stuck in the cramped space. It was hypnotic: The dog would take the same amount of steps, turn, then take the same number in the opposite direction. It was if he were a machine, each move consistent, precise. He wondered if it followed the same route, night after night, never going anywhere.

"Hey, Marlborough Man!" a voice shouted out from behind Kyle. Kyle turned reluctantly away from the dog to look in the direction of the voice.

Something hit him — hard. The buildings seemed to spin around, the snow-covered concrete rushed at him. Only reflex made him bring up his hands in time to brace himself, stopping his face from slamming against the cold pavement. Slowly, he forced himself up on his knees.

"Remember me, Marlborough Man?" The voice was far off, muffled. Kyle felt something warm run across his cold cheeks. A mist had formed around him and everything seemed to slow down. He felt the cold concrete seep through his jeans, numbing his knees. He found it hard to collect his thoughts, to figure out what had happened to him. Then, a heavy boot swung out of the fog. He tried to move out of the way but felt the jarring pain as it sunk into his ribs. The air rushed from his lungs and Kyle toppled over. Drops of blood, his own blood, melted quickly into the snow below his head. The kick seemed to chase away the fog, bring his senses back sharply. His head throbbed madly, worse than the pain in his side as he drew his arms around his head, pulling his knees up instinctively, trying to protect himself from the next blow. It wasn't long in coming.

Kyle looked up at the punks surrounding him. Now he remembered where he had seen them before. Two of them were the kids he had chased from the phone booth last week.

"You remember, don't you?" the green-haired kid asked. He was wearing the same clothes he had worn that night. His friend's arms were still bare beneath the frayed jean jacket.

"Time to pay the fine," No-sleeves said. Kyle somehow noticed the kid had lost a front tooth since the last time they had met. He felt a few more kicks in his back and arms. It hurt, but he had been hurt worse in football. Still, Kyle knew that he had to do something quickly, the beating would only get worse. He saw that the green-haired boy held the end of a broken baseball bat. He assumed that was what they had hit him with first. The green-haired boy laughed while his associates took turns kicking.

"Give up the money!" one of the others yelled. Kyle didn't know which. He guessed they had watched him pay his bill.

Seeing his chance, he reached out and grabbed the leg of one of his attackers, just as his boot came flying toward Kyle. He pulled hard and the attacker lost his balance on the icy concrete, crashing into Green-hair. Both of them tumbled heavily to the ground. Using the split second he had given himself as the other two stared, Kyle scrambled to his feet. His entire body ached, and his head spun as he stood to his full height, swinging his arms around wildly, hoping to hit one of his attackers.

"Get him!" Green-hair shouted. He, too, was scrambling to his feet.

No-sleeves jumped on Kyle's back and hung on like a wild animal, screaming and scratching at his face and eyes. Across the street the Doberman was barking hysterically. Kyle began screaming as well, in anger as well as pain, swinging the bare-armed kid around to shake him off. He felt the thud and a surge of pleasure as one of No-sleeves' boots hit Green-hair squarely in the jaw. Kyle twisted and spun, nearly losing his balance as No-sleeves finally let go, flying in mid-air and landing heavily in a pile of snow and ice. Free at last, Kyle stood upright, ready for the next attack. Green-hair and the others stood up as well, about to charge Kyle. He knew that he should run, that he had almost no hope against these odds. He also knew that the chances were good that despite his speed, he'd still be caught. Then Green-hair and the others hesitated. They began to back off, slowly. Puzzled, Kyle waited, wondering what had frightened them. Just then, Green-hair turned on his heels and ran. The others were close behind.

The danger from his attackers suddenly gone, Kyle turned to find out just what had scared them off. From the shadows of the building behind him he saw a dark figure emerge, then another, and another. Ten or so kids walked through the snow toward him. Kyle felt really afraid now. Something about these silent, dark figures frightened him more than the punks. They surrounded him quickly, boys and girls. At least two of them held knives, he saw the glint of sharp steel in their hands, arms hanging loosely at their sides. The night was strangely silent now and he wondered why. Then he remembered the huge black dog across the street. He glanced quickly to his right and saw it had stopped pacing and stared down at Kyle and the others. In the cold air, the dog's breath rose in tight, quick clouds that drifted quickly away.

"I hear you've been asking questions. Looking for me," a voice said. It was a girl's voice, clear and soft, but with an edge that Kyle found disturbing.

Kyle looked down as the girl stepped out of the shadows toward him. Her black hair hung in her eyes and she pulled it back as she looked up at him. Her skin was a dull white, her eyes elaborately made up. Her lips were blood red and a single teardrop was tattooed under the orbit of her right eye. Across her pale neck, a strangely shaped cross hung on a thick chain. She was smoking and he saw the hand that held the cigarette was decorated in a delicate spider web pattern. He wasn't sure if it was make-up or another tattoo. Kyle recognized her instantly, even though she had only been an entry in Meghan's diary. Janice.

"I need you to help me," Kyle said. "To find my sister. She's on the street."

"There's a lot of girls on the street." Janice began to turn away, blowing smoke in Kyle's face and he felt panic, seeing his best hope slip away.

"Her name is Meghan."

Janice stopped and looked up at him, then at the others. She looked at the patch on his team jacket that read Perry, just as Meghan's had. Janice nodded slightly and the others slipped their knives away. Like Janice, they all wore black, their faces looking as pale and as cool as the ice beneath them. At least, the faces he could actually see. Most of them were still in the shadows. One of the girls was familiar: He thought she was the one who swore at him in the park last week. She still held her knife out, ready. Her make-up, even her tattoo were too similar to Janice's to be coincidence. The girl was obviously imitating her. There was no sign of the little girl with the red mark over her lip.

"What makes you think I know anything?"

"I don't know. Not for sure," Kyle said. "I don't have anyone else to ask."

Janice looked at him. Her eyes were a pale, pale blue. For some reason this surprised Kyle. He hadn't expected her to have blue eyes.

"She'll come home. When she's tired of playing," Janice said.

"It's been over a month and no one's heard a thing from her."

Janice seemed to study him closely, thinking.

"There's a boarded-up parking lot across from the Tower, on 9th. You know it?"

"I can find it," Kyle said.

"What are you doin'!" the young girl shouted, stepping up to Janice. She stopped in mid-sentence when Janice glared at her. The girl glared back at Kyle.

"You find a way in, you'll find us," Janice said. "Tomorrow. Past midnight."

Kyle nodded. Janice said nothing else, just turned away as she and the others began to disappear.

Before she joined them, the girl who had spoken up crouched in front of Kyle. Extending her index finger, she scooped up some of the snow stained with Kyle's blood. Staring into his eyes the whole time, she stood as she stuck the finger in her mouth. Without a word, she turned and joined the others in the shadows.

Kyle stood there watching where they had disappeared until he heard the dog begin to bark again. He shivered and realized that his jacket had been torn open in the fight. His head began to throb where he had been hit by the broken bat, the muscles around his back and arms had already begun to ache and stiffen. He bent down and grabbed a handful of snow to wipe the blood from his face. He turned to walk north toward the commuter train station, holding a chunk of ice to the cut on his forehead. It quickly stemmed the bleeding. As he walked, he thought of his mother's reaction when he finally arrived home, hours late and bleeding. Kyle thought he knew the exact words she would use.

He was wrong.

***

Kyle turned the key in the lock and stepped inside the house as quietly as possible. He was hoping that his mother had gone to bed and that he could postpone the inevitable until morning. Instead, all the lights were on and the radio was playing softly in the living room. Kyle knew that he would have to face her now instead of later.

Taking a deep breath, Kyle walked down the short hall to the living room. He knew she was in for a shock when she saw him.

"What the hell happened to you?" It was a different voice than the one he expected.

Kyle stopped dead, felt the blood drain from his face. His mother was sitting on the couch, sipping coffee, just as he had pictured. There was only one thing wrong with the scene.

There on their worn couch, wearing the usual expensive suit, sat his father.

# Chapter 8

"Nice of you to come home," his father said, when Kyle walked in the room. It had been several months since they had last spoken and this was his greeting. Kyle wished that he had been able to clean himself up better, that the whole evening could have been different. He had always hated looking ridiculous in front of his father.

"What happened to you?" his mother asked, jumping up from the couch, her coffee cup clutched in her hand, forgotten.

"Nothing," Kyle said, shaking his head. "I had an accident."

"Some accident," his father replied. "Do all your accidents wear boots?"

Kyle looked down at his jacket. It still had a few filthy marks left from the beating. Boot prints were easily legible. "I better go clean up."

His mother had replaced the coffee cup on the tray and rushed to Kyle, checking him over. "Are you hurt badly?" she asked, running her hand through his short hair, examining every cut and bruise.

"Nothing serious. I ran into some punks, that's all."

"You could have been killed!" his mother exclaimed. "I've seen it on the news. These street gangs are vicious. They kill kids just for their jackets!"

"The boy can handle himself, Laura," his father said.

"How does he handle himself against a gun?"

"Would you cut it out?" Kyle said. "It was nothing! No gang! No guns! Just a couple of punks looking for a fight."

His mother still looked worried. He could see she was appraising the damage to her son.

"Your team jacket is ruined," she said finally. "And it took you so long to save for it."

Kyle looked away from her, feeling a rush of guilt. It contrasted with the rush of anger he felt, seeing his father smirk at her innocent remark. Both of them, father and son, knew where the money had really come from.

"I'm going to clean up," Kyle said, walking away.

"Do that," his father said. "Then you can tell your mother and I more about what you think you're doing every night."

After a hot shower and a change of clothes, dragging it out as long as possible, Kyle joined his parents in the living room. It seemed as if they hadn't moved, but a fresh pot of coffee sat on the table between them. Kyle and his mother made brief eye contact as he entered, and he saw anger there. He wasn't sure just who she was most angry with. She looked at the gauze he had expertly taped to his forehead. After all the years of sports, he was no stranger to cuts and bruises.

"So," his father said as Kyle sat on the only other chair, nibbling from a cookie he had picked up as he passed. Kyle saw him examine him as he entered the room. He seemed to satisfy himself that the fight had left no permanent injuries. He moved on to the real subject of his visit. "Now that we're all here, who wants to tell me why it has taken this long to find out my daughter has been running wild?"

"I already explained it to you, Robert," Kyle's mother began. "It hasn't been that long and we're doing all that we can ..."

"So just when were you planning on telling me? When they brought her home in a body bag?"

"That's a horrible thing to say!" his mother said. Kyle saw the colour drain from her face. He felt his own initial discomfort begin to turn to anger. Nothing had changed. There was no middle ground with his father.

"Who told you?" Kyle asked.

"Surprisingly enough, my dear ex-mother-in-law!"

"My mother called you?"

Kyle's father looked at his ex-wife, his face perfectly calm. He drained the last drop of coffee from his cup. "Seems that she's very worried about the way you're raising our children," he continued. "Now that I'm here, I can see why."

Kyle wasn't sure if his father was referring to him, what had happened with Meghan or the state of the house they lived in. Probably all three. And more.

"She started ranting about how I should pay more attention to my daughter's behaviour. What kind of father was I? How could I abandon my family? Other garbage. I had to hang up on her. By the way, is that what you tell people? That I abandoned my family?"

Kyle's mother sipped her coffee, refusing to look at him. She glanced at Kyle, then looked slowly around at the shabby room. "I don't have to tell people anything."

"How could you afford to come out here, Dad?" Kyle asked before his father could start again. "I thought you had lost everything?"

His father shot him a look and leaned over to fill his cup once more.

"I get by. And besides, my daughter's safety is the most important thing right now!" He sat back on the couch and looked at his son, taking another sip of his coffee. Despite his anger Kyle noticed that his father somehow made the old couch look even more worn out.

The conversation turned back to Meghan, his father wanting to know what had happened — "brought up to speed" was the phrase he used. It was one of many pet sayings that peppered any conversation he had. Kyle had loved to use them himself when he was younger, when his father had seemed so strong, so flawless. They had been imbedded for so long that he still found one or two popping out.

These days, he made more and more of an effort to erase them from his vocabulary.

Kyle soon discovered that his father had arrived at the house that evening unannounced, after spending the day hounding the police officers in charge of the case. He was convinced that finally real action would take place, now that Robert C. Perry was involved. It was only a matter of time before Meghan was home and everything was back to whatever passed for normal these days. Besides, he was willing to pound the streets himself. He knew how to get these street types to talk. He outlined his plans, the first being that, starting tomorrow night, they would begin to check the streets themselves. All three of them.

"First we'll have dinner at my hotel. Then Kyle here can show us where to start looking."

"I can't," Kyle's mother replied. "I have work to do."

"You can't take one night off to search for your daughter?"

"I don't need to explain myself to you," she replied. "And I don't need you to show up to organize our lives. We've done fine without you."

"Really?" he asked. "Then tell me, Laura. Where is Meghan? Why did she run away? And what exactly has your son been up to every night?"

Kyle shifted uncomfortably in his chair. He knew what was coming, had seen the same scene act itself out over and over again. It was the way his parents always acted.

"Forget it," he said. "I don't want to hear this again. I'm going to bed."

"That's it?" his father asked sarcastically. "You haven't seen me in months and you can't stay up an extra five minutes to talk?"

Kyle stood up, feeling his muscles begin to cramp. He knew that he would be sore for several days. There were so many replies he could have made, but he decided to stop himself. It was a well-known fact in the family that in any argument with Dad, you could only lose. Without a word, Kyle waved and headed down the hall to his room. As he got ready for bed, he could still hear the low murmur of his parents' discussion.

Much later, a terrible headache woke Kyle. He stumbled down the hall toward the bathroom, looking for an aspirin, then stopped suddenly. A light was still on in the living room. He crept down the hall quietly, and saw by the kitchen clock that it was past three. Peering around the corner, he saw his mother sitting on the couch, her feet curled up beneath her. She held an old photo album in her lap, but she wasn't looking at it. Instead, she seemed to be staring off at the far wall, lost in her thoughts. He saw the tears run freely down her cheeks. Kyle turned away, as silently as he had come, not wanting her to see him.

# Chapter 9

October 15

Dear Me,

Sorry to have been neglecting you again old diary, but life's been moving along and I don't have as much free time as I used to. Thank God! It looks like the last entry was a week ago, detailing my first night staying with Stephen. I better make sure my mom never reads *that* little entry.

I haven't been writing because I'd rather be out doing stuff than be stuck at home writing about the stuff I wish I was doing. Right now, I'm actually not at home. Yes, folks, this diary entry is coming to you live/*en direct* from the bedroom of my first real boyfriend, Stephen! The only bad part about it is that he's not home right now, either. Which is okay, too, 'cause I'm pretty tired. All that partying can sure tucker a girl out!

Let's see ... it is almost 5 a.m. and Stephen's been gone about two hours or so. There was another party here tonight and the usual gang showed up. Lots of them are still here, passed out on the floor outside. The stereo is still playing, someone put on a Metallica CD and must have put it on repeat before they passed out — it's played about ten times now. I'm surprised the neighbours don't call the cops — it's so loud here all the time. Then again, I suppose I'm not that surprised, you should see the neighbours! One of them was carried out of here by the paramedics — her husband or boyfriend or whatever he is had stuck a huge knife in her stomach. They were both so high or drunk that they were still yelling at each other when she was being loaded into the ambulance. The knife kind of jumped around when she screamed. Pretty gross, huh? It was kind of neat, too. Like a horror movie or something.

I've seen a lot of awful things in the last month or so, since I started seeing Stephen. The crowd he hangs around with can be rough. A lot of them are street kids or people who lived on the streets. There's a lot of parties and drinking and drugs. Most of these people don't seem to have jobs so I don't know how they live. Stephen's place seems to be the hangout for most of them. He lets them stay here for a while then tells them to clear out. I think some of them sell drugs and some of the girls are hookers. They're pretty messed up, and Stephen doesn't like me to talk to them. He keeps me separate from them when he can.

I've also met his boss, A.J. (everyone just calls him Age). I have no idea what his real name is. He really creeps me out. I know he helps Stephen a lot, gives him extra cash when he needs it and other things. I think he even pays the rent here (I'm not sure, just something I overheard.) It's a strange relationship. Of course, he makes Stephen work all kinds of weird hours doing who knows what. I'm pretty sure that whatever he's doing, it's not all legal. Not that Stephen's a crook or anything — I think he's just doing what he's told to do by Age.

I made Stephen put a lock on the bedroom door. People have just wandered in when we're here. A couple of times they came in when I was alone. I've also told him that Age has come on to me a few times. He always tries to get me alone, standing too close, touching my hair and stuff. He's really gross. Fat, balding, greasy. He looks like a biker, really tough. Stephen says he's just trying to be nice, to get to know me. I'd rather he not get to know me too well, if you know what I mean.

I heard them arguing about something one night after I had told Stephen that Age was bugging me again. They were out on the street, and Age was in his car, so I didn't hear too well, but it sounded like Stephen was sticking up for me. Age said something that shut him up, and he looked a little worried when he came back inside.

I may be getting a little melodramatic, but I've figured out a way of getting out of here quickly if I have to. There's a window in the bedroom that faces the back alley. We're only on the second floor and right below is one of those big garbage bins. It's usually full so I think I can jump into it without hurting myself too badly. Let's hope I don't have to ever do it, but it doesn't hurt to plan ahead, in case. There's something about Age that worries me.

Okay, I'm creeped out, a little worried, but Stephen's still great. He drinks a little too much, maybe does too much dope, but who can blame him? He's had a pretty tough life and I think Age makes him do a lot of stuff he doesn't really want to do. And okay, when Stephen gets too high he can get mean. Once, when he was complaining about Age, I asked him why he couldn't get another job. He just laughed at me, and so did some of the others.

"Sometimes I forget how dumb you are!" he said to me. I couldn't believe it! I felt so horrible — he made me look so stupid in front of everyone! Later on, he was all sorry and apologetic, of course, but I still felt hurt. There's been a couple of other things that worried me, but, hey, no relationship's perfect, right? Just ask Mom and Pop.

Speaking of which, as you might have guessed, I don't spend a lot of time at home these days. Or at school. It's so lame anyway. Mom was just riding me all the time, trying to ground me, to make me go to school. She even called the cops when I didn't come home for three or four days. Stephen tells me not to worry, there's nothing the cops can do. There's no law that lets your parents make you stay at home or go to school. In fact, if they try to keep you at home, or lock you in your room to stop you from going on the street, they can get charged! He says I can pretty well do what I want and no one can stop me. I don't know if it's really true or not, but so far that's how it's been. Sometimes I think I should go home, but then I think of how my mother will react — she'll tell me not to see Stephen and go to school or whatever. Who needs the hassle? At least here no one tells me what to do.

I do get bored sometimes, maybe a little lonely. Stephen is away a lot, in the afternoons and evenings. I wander around downtown, look at the stuff in stores. I think I even miss school a little. Can you believe that? I know I miss my books and going to movies, hanging out with friends. None of Stephen's friends are the kind I'd like to hang out with for very long. He doesn't read books or watch movies. He thinks his life is better than a movie. Maybe he's right.

Wandering around downtown has made me see just how many other kids are skipping or living on the streets. There's a ton of them! I can recognize the street kids now. They look tougher, and they always wear the same clothes and carry backpacks. Probably that's where they keep their stuff.

I've seen Janice and her gang a lot. Never in daylight, always in the evening or late at night. I've even followed them around, making sure they don't notice me. They shoplift and steal money from the drunks on Electric Avenue, do all kinds of things. They remind me of a pack of wild animals, never doing stuff alone, just moving, staying alive. I hope I never end up like them.

I've even seen where they live, this old abandoned parking building. Late at night, you can see flames flickering behind the windows that are still in place. Creepy, huh? Stephen knows about them.

He told me they think they really are vampires, that the new kids have to drink the leaders' blood to join. Can you believe someone actually doing that? Stephen knows a lot about these gangs of kids that survive on the street. It's a pretty small world and everyone seems to know about everyone else. Even if it's only by reputation. It seems that reputation is the most important thing on the street. Sometimes it's the only thing that keeps you alive. One thing you don't do is cross another gang. People can actually get killed for doing that.

Now that I've met Age, I think I know what Janice was trying to tell me that day at the Gardens. He is someone to watch out for.

The stereo just shut off and I hear Stephen yelling, tossing out some of the crashers. Time to go! I don't know why, but I don't want him or anyone else to know that I'm writing this diary. I've got a great hiding spot for it.

See ya!

— Meghan

# Chapter 10

Kyle looked up at the Calgary Tower, watching the lights flash, his eyes following the flicker of the torch burning at the top, glowing in the ice fog that had descended once more on the city. The flame reflected on the glass-enclosed walkway that led to the abandoned parkade, the place where Janice had told him to meet her. He wandered around the building, seeing that the first three floors were boarded up tight, sheets of plywood covering every entrance. A few windows at the higher levels were still intact and also caught some of the light from the tower. Old posters and handbills littered the boards, as well as the usual spray-painted graffiti. "Juice Rools!" one read; others said "The End is Near!" "John 3.16" and "Age is the Enemi!" He had seen that last message before, done in the same perfect lettering. This time he understood its significance.

Earlier, after a wonderful meal at the Palliser, his father's hotel, the three of them left to cruise the streets in his father's rented car. Kyle felt some guilt at enjoying the meal and being with his parents in luxurious surroundings once again. It had been so long since he had eaten like this. He wondered if his mother felt the same way, and if so, if she felt the same guilt at enjoying it so much.

The evening had been a disaster after that. It was ridiculous, really. The huge car pulling to the side of the street, his father waving money and a picture of Meghan, asking some poor, skinny kid if he had seen her. Most of the kids, desperate for money, had lied, leading them to another street, another coffee shop or drop-in centre, another dead end. They had all seen her, they assured his father, last night, this morning, or by sheer luck, only hours before. You couldn't miss her! She was there, definitely! She never was.

It had warmed up slightly since last night, but he had been on the street for over half an hour now since leaving the C-Train station and the cold was beginning to seep through his clothes. He had waited until after his father had left, driving his fancy rented car back to the hotel downtown. Most people would take cabs in a city they barely knew, but not his father. He liked to be in control, and to make a show of his own competence. When his mother had gone to her room, Kyle had sneaked quietly out the back door, wearing his oldest clothes. He didn't want to stand out, to chance a repeat of last night's attack.

And now it was past midnight and traffic was light along 9th Avenue. Cabs pulled away from the hotel that sat directly across from the tower's main entrance. A white police car slowed to a crawl when the officers inside spotted Kyle walking slowly along the street. He tried to act casual, as if he were out for a stroll, just heading back to the hotel. He relaxed finally as the car sped away, the cops obviously deciding he was of no concern. When they were out of sight, he turned and walked down the alley behind the parkade.

Here too, Kyle saw the building was boarded up with plywood and chains. Rusted metal sheets were bolted firmly to what was once the exit ramp. He looked up and saw no other way in on the higher levels. Frustrated, he wondered if Janice had just told him to meet her here to get rid of him. He could almost hear them, sitting someplace warm, laughing at the big, stupid jock!

Now Kyle stood freezing in the cold night, alone in a desolate alley, feeling like a fool. Another dead end! Tomorrow night, he would have to start the search with his father once again. Fed up, he began to turn, to head back to the street and then home. Something caught his eye and he stopped. He had passed a huge blue garbage bin that had been slammed against the side of the building, probably acting as one more barricade. Beside it he saw something unusual, hardly visible in the poor light the one and only streetlamp offered. He crouched down and pushed away the piles of garbage bags that had collected there. Most of them looked frozen and snow covered, obviously left there for some time. But Kyle saw that a few were curiously free of snow. He pulled them aside and peered into the darkness. There was a rusted metal grating there, the covering of a vent once used to heat the building. Kyle saw that the hinges were rusted as well, and that a thick latch held the grate shut. He pulled on it, expecting it to be as secure as it looked. To his surprise, the grate and the rusted latch lifted easily up. Positioning himself better, he pushed, straining to lift the thick metal grate up. It took all his strength to lift it and he knew that someone like Janice would need others to help. His muscles ached as he shifted his weight once more. He felt the pain in his ribs flare where the boots had landed only last night.

Bracing the grate with one arm, Kyle slipped into the darkness below.

***

It was slightly warmer in here, wherever it was Kyle stood, but the smell was sickening. And it was pitch black. He reached into his jacket pocket and pulled out the pack of matches he had taken from the Palliser dining room earlier. At the time, they had been a souvenir, an old habit of his. Now they would prove useful. He lit a match and looked quickly around in its weak light before it sputtered out, burning his thumb. The light had been bad, but it had been enough to give an impression of the size of the small area, and he thought he recognized something else. Kyle groped around in the darkness, thankful that it was winter and that whatever objects he was touching were frozen solid. Finally, on a narrow ledge of the wall in front of him, he touched something that felt useful. Striking another match, he held it close to the object he held. It was a box of candles. Obviously he had found the entrance.

After some more fumbling, Kyle held the lit candle in front of him and looked around. He was in a small, concrete chamber, about five feet square and about the same in height. He had to crouch to avoid hitting the grate above his head. His cold feet disappeared in a mound of torn garbage bags, cardboard, yellowed newspapers and some kind of dead animal, unrecognizable now. To his left, he saw a small opening, about a metre or so high. Replacing the box of candles, he knelt down and looked inside. The walls here were also concrete and the candle only lit a few feet ahead, before it plunged once more into shadow. There was a foul odour coming from the space. Breathing only through his mouth, Kyle began to crawl forward, knowing there was no other place to go. Inching along, he felt his back and shoulders scrape against the narrow walls and was glad he had decided to wear old clothes. They would be trashed after this.

At last, Kyle stood up straight after pulling himself free of the narrow tunnel. He was on the first level of the parkade, his footsteps echoing hollowly in the huge, empty spaces. He had no idea how long the place had been abandoned, but he could still smell motor oil and exhaust fumes imbedded permanently into the cold concrete walls.

Kyle wanted to call out, to let whoever was here know he had made it inside. Some sense told him to stay quiet, that shouting was the wrong thing to do. There was more light here, spilling through cracks in the wooden sheets used to seal the building and the tiny smashed windows above them. To his right, he saw a doorway, with a sign above it that still read STREET LEVEL: ACCESS TO 9TH AVENUE S.E. Shifting the candle to his left hand, he pulled on the metal bar. The door stayed shut, locked tight.

Kyle looked around and saw the circular ramps that cars had once used. He began climbing the ice-covered slope, looking up at the curving levels disappearing into darkness above him. He thought he caught a glimpse of something moving up there, watching him. Whatever he saw was gone quickly and he suspected it was just his imagination.

He kept climbing up the slippery incline, looking at the scraped sides of the wall, the painted signs that told him where he was: LEVEL 2, LEVEL 3, LEVEL 4 AND WALKWAY TO HUSKY TOWER. Even a newcomer like Kyle knew that it had been years since the Calgary Tower had been called that. He found it harder to climb the further he walked; the incline and the foul air were exhausting.

"That's far enough!" a voice shouted from above. Kyle looked up, startled, his breath billowing around his head in the cold air, making it even more difficult to see.

"I'm looking for Janice!" he shouted back in the direction of the voice. "My name's Kyle!"

"We know who you are," another voice said. A girl's voice this time, almost right beside him. He thought he recognized it. Kyle spun around. Two

figures in black stood at the edge of the ramp looking down at him. One was a male, slightly smaller
than Kyle. He thought it was the same boy he had
seen hiding in the shadows last night.

"Otherwise you wouldn't have made it this far,"
the girl said. She stepped slightly closer and Kyle
saw he was right — it was the girl who had ob-
jected when Janice had told him where they lived.
She jerked her head slightly before turning to walk
away. Kyle followed, up one more ramp.

They walked farther inside, past concrete barri-
ers to the second level of this floor. There was a huge
doorway there, its shut doors almost three metres
high. MAINTENANCE VEHICLES ONLY was
painted on one door, faded and peeling like the rest
of the signs. The tall boy pulled on the door with
both hands and it swung open with less effort than
Kyle would have guessed. He suspected that the
hinges had been oiled, protected from the elements.

Kyle walked inside, once more following the
girl. He felt the difference in temperature immediately. It was much warmer here, and the high walls
and ceilings were bathed in a yellowish, flickering
light. He heard the door slam shut behind and sensed
that the tall boy now stood beside him. Kyle stepped
a little farther inside. The first thing he noticed was
the loud music and how bright the place was. As
he walked on, he saw that the room was lit by
dozens of candles, stuck on the pipes that had once
run water and heat through the building. A five-
pointed star was painted on the back wall, upside
down and in blood red paint. Graffiti was painted

everywhere, some crude, some beautiful. A kind of mural was painted on the side wall. Dark figures, with more than a passing resemblance to the gang, glared eerily out of a veil of mist. Even to Kyle's untrained eye, the mural was beautiful. In the centre was a girl, a gold circle shimmering behind her head, like a halo from some old religious painting. White wings spread out behind her: a goth angel. He studied the face for a moment and noticed that the rough concrete surface of the wall added something to the painting. It made the girl's face look like that of a carved angel, the kind he had seen in a graveyard years before.

Kyle looked around him. Clothes that had been halfheartedly washed hung on wire lines stretched between concrete pillars. They were drying over a huge bonfire blazing in a shallow pit in the centre of the room. A dozen or so kids lay around it, propped up on old bits of furniture, frayed and torn couches and chairs, sleeping bags, and dirty blankets. They were in couples or sat a bit apart, alone. All of them watched Kyle through hooded eyes, wary and bored at the same time. He saw Janice sitting near the fire in an overstuffed chair, cradling a sleeping girl in her lap. He saw it was the same silent girl he had seen begging in the park. A library of sorts, boxes spilling over with old books, lay beside the chair. He wondered if Janice had read them all.

"I see you found the place all right," Janice said as Kyle approached her. She spoke gently, perhaps to avoid waking the sleeping child. Kyle saw other kids asleep as well, scattered about like the blankets. None of them were as young as the one in Janice's lap. He almost smiled at her greeting, as if they were in the suburbs and he had merely dropped in for coffee.

Kyle nodded. "Yeah, but I think my jacket's finished."

"Poor boy!" the girl who had led him said. The others laughed as she walked away and lay down on a pile of sleeping bags. Janice grinned as well, slipping herself away from the sleeping girl, laying her head down gently on the chair. She walked over to a battered fridge propped against a wall, its door long gone. Kyle followed her, all too aware of others watching him intently.

"You hungry? Thirsty?"

He was both. But he looked at the condition of the place, the foul odours, and the dirt, and decided he better ignore his hunger. He shook his head at the offered beer.

"Come on," Janice said. "It's not polite to refuse our hospitality."

Kyle wasn't sure if she was being sarcastic like her friend. He decided to accept the drink, hoping that the alcohol would kill anything that might be growing on the bottle. Janice took another beer and twisted off the top, taking a long sip. She nodded toward the fire and they walked back to it. It was noticeably colder even a few feet farther away from the flames.

"So," she said as they hunkered down at the edge of the pit, staring into the fire. Kyle glanced over at her as she watched the flames, her white skin reflecting the orange glow. He looked up, wondering where the smoke escaped. The ceiling disappeared into the gloom. The mural once more caught his eye. The figures on it seemed to move, to watch him. Kyle found it creepy, even though it was just a trick of the light.

"Why are you looking for your sister?"

Kyle was shocked by the question. It wasn't what he was expecting.

"Why not?" he replied, thinking quickly. "She's my *sister*."

"That's supposed to explain it?" Janice asked. She stared at him, just as she had last night, like she could see under his skin. No one had looked at him in quite this way before.

"She's family. And she's all alone on the street."

"No one's alone on the street," a tall boy said. It was the first time Kyle had heard him speak. He looked over and saw that the boy sat on the sleeping bags, slipping an arm around the girl. He too, had grabbed a beer.

"So you love her?" Janice said. "That's the reason you want to find her?"

"I guess so," Kyle replied, embarrassed by the directness of the question. Love wasn't a word used much in his family.

"Exactly how do you love her?" the girl who looked like Janice asked. Kyle looked over at her and saw she wasn't smiling. She looked at him as directly as Janice had.

"What do you mean?" Kyle asked.

"She means were you messing around with her? Is that why she ran?" The boy looked at him coldly.

"Are you sick?" Kyle shouted. "She's my sister for God's sake!"

"Sister, daughter, cousin, niece. The little girl who lives down the street ..." the girl on the sleeping bags chanted. Kyle looked away from her, embarrassed and angry at the same time.

Janice grinned and looked over at the girl.

"I don't think this is funny," Kyle said, offended.

Janice shrugged. "Sorry. I was just quoted," she said. Kyle had no idea what she was talking about.

"Not much surprises us down here," the girl said, looking at Kyle. "You can tell us anything."

"Just like confession time at church," the tall boy said, laughing. Some of the others laughed too.

Kyle looked around at them, wondering if they were all crazy. He began to think that he had made yet another wrong choice. He stood up quickly, dropping the beer bottle on the concrete floor.

"Careful," the girl said. "There's a deposit on that!"

"Maybe you just slapped her around once in a while," Janice asked. "You know, when she needed it?"

"I never touched Meghan! Maybe I wasn't the greatest brother or anything, but ..." he stopped, too angry to think clearly, to form the words he wanted to say.

"Relax," Janice said. "We just wanted to know." Kyle wanted to say something, but he was interrupted when six or seven of the others, boys and girls, stood and began to walk toward the doors.

"It's time," one of them said to Janice. She nodded.

"Watch yourselves. Stay together."

"Piece of cake," the boy replied, shrugging. They filed out silently, closing the doors behind them. Kyle felt a blast of cold wind as the doors were opened. He shivered, despite the heat from the flames. He wondered how people could survive in that kind of cold for very long.

"Sit down," the girl on the sleeping bag said, snuggling closer to the tall boy, taking a sip of his beer. "Stay awhile." They both laughed at this. Kyle didn't get the joke.

"Let me tell you a story," Janice said, holding out her hand to him.

# Chapter 11

October 25

I've got to write this fast, there's not a lot of time left now. I'm cold and miserable and I don't know what to do. Things have got too strange in the last few days. I still can't believe how stupid I've been. Serves me right, I guess. I'm the one who had all the answers. Right?

So now, I'm on the run from Age! And from Stephen!

Remember him, Dear Diary? The love of my life? Seems that he wasn't entirely honest with me, to put it mildly. Turns out his name isn't really Stephen, that's just his street name. He really did name himself after the mall, just like he told me the day I met him. Who knows what his real name is? Who cares? He's a recruiter, a sleazeball who works for a pimp gathering up stupid, gullible girls like me to work the streets. Isn't that sick? And I fell for it!

Everything's fallen apart so fast it's hard for me to figure out what happened.

The last few nights I've been on the street alone. Good thing I paid attention, so I know a lot of the places you can sleep without being raped or beaten, or waking up dead. And, of course, it's the worst October in Calgary in 50 years or something. It's so cold out here! They're packing frozen street people off to the morgue every other day. Not much choice for me though. If I don't stay hidden and moving, it won't be the cold that finishes me off.

I can't go home either. Stephen knows where I live. He'll find me there. And God knows what Age would do to my family if they happened to be home when he called. I know this all sounds like a bad TV movie. But it's happening.

One thing's for sure — they won't get me. I'm still smarter than all of them.

I have one chance, I think. Janice. If I can find her, I think she might help me get out of the city. People are kind of scared of her and her gang. They're into drinking blood and black magic and stuff. A couple of months ago I wouldn't have believed a story like that. Now, I believe people are capable of anything. I've seen it.

***

October 29

It's my ninth, maybe tenth day on the street. Last night, I even tried calling home. I figured what have I got to lose? No answer, of course, just the machine. I hung up. This morning, I panhandled enough money to get a hamburger and a ticket for the LRT. I was

94

going to sneak into my house, get some new clothes, some real food and a hot shower (I smell really, really bad). I got on the train on Seventh, but guess what? Some of Age's goofs were hanging around the station. I was so scared! They almost caught me!

Then tonight, I finally found Janice.

Maybe I should say she found me. Turns out she knew what had happened to me, that I was on the run. She had been looking for me. She and her gang squat in this old abandoned parking lot. That's where I am now. It smells bad in here, like exhaust fumes and dead animals or something. They've got a fire going, so it's not so cold, although you freeze if you move more than ten feet away from the flames. I'm bundled up under a pile of smelly blankets and a sleeping bag, so I'm not too bad. I'm writing this by candlelight, which, by the way, isn't easy. The words kind of dance around every time there's even a bit of a breeze. Her gang looks pretty creepy, but they're okay. I heard Janice arguing with one of them, an older boy. I think he was afraid that I would get them in trouble or something. I think he's afraid of Age. Can't say I blame him.

Right now, Janice and the others are out roaming the streets. I've seen what they do out there. I think they panhandle, roll a few drunks, sell a little dope. You know. Just kids having fun. They must also scrounge around for stuff to keep the fire going. It doesn't take long for cardboard and old wooden skids to burn. They left me with the little girl, the one I saw before at the Devonian Gardens. I guess she must be eight or nine. She's asleep now, look-ing really cute, despite the fact she's as white as a sheet and her hair is greasy and dyed jet black. She has this weird birthmark under her nose, like a little red moustache. Since Janice brought me here about four or five hours ago, the kid's never said a word. She just looks at you. It's weird, but of all of them, she's the one that freaks me out the most. It's just not normal for a kid that age never to make a sound. While they were gone, I found a notebook in Janice's things. I thought it was a diary, like mine. It's a bunch of poems and stuff. Some of it's really good, too. As much as I can tell anyway. I've seen this a lot. Girls on the streets write poems. I guess it's one way of sharing their feelings.

"You should just go home," Janice told me.

"I can't," I said. "Stephen and Age would find me there. I'd always be afraid they'd get me."

"They won't chase you back there. What's in it for them?"

I was a little ticked at that. Who'd she think she was? And anyway, if they wanted me that badly before, why stop now? I said something about how embarrassing it would be to go back to school now, after being on the street. Kids would treat me like a freak.

"You mean like me?" Janice asked.

"Yeah," I said. "Like you."

"You're nothing like me," Janice said.

I had a few more things to say to her. One thing I've learned these past weeks is not to let anyone give you any crap. But I figured it was best to drop it. She was letting me stay here. And she finally agreed to get me out of the city. She says she knows someone heading out to Vancouver in a couple of days. She'll see what she can do to get them to take me along. I can hardly wait! Vancouver! Can you imagine? It's warm and there's the ocean and the island and I know I can get my life together once I get away from here. I'm smart. And I can take care of myself!

# Chapter 12

"So what happened next?"

"You tell me," Janice replied. "You've got the diary."

"That's the last entry."

Kyle lay the tattered notebook down between them and stared at it for a moment. It was the only thing that still tied him to Meghan. It was weird how a few words, scribbled hastily in a book, had brought him closer to his sister than all the years they had lived together. For the first time he saw her as a person, not just his annoying little sister. He hoped that their troubles would be over soon, so that they could get back to their lives.

"Like I said," Janice said, yawning. "She never showed. None of us've seen her since."

"How can you be so calm? She didn't just disappear. Someone must know where she is!" Kyle was getting angry at her relaxed attitude. She knew better than anyone what kind of danger Meghan was in. Janice just looked away, taking a long sip of her beer.

Kyle stood up and started to pace. He gazed into the fire, then at the shadowy figures huddled together in the darkness beyond the firelight. Most of the candles had flickered out in the cold breeze that occasionally blasted through the room. No one bothered to light them again.

"It's past one," the boy on the sleeping bags said. Kyle knew his name now, Shadow, and his girlfriend was called Smoke. He had picked up that piece of information through their conversation.

"Showtime!" Smoke said, rising to her feet. She adjusted her clothes, then lifted her cloak, pulling a long, deadly looking blade from a sheath sewn into the lining. Kyle wondered if she did this for his benefit. She looked up, catching him stare at the knife as she slipped it precisely in place.

"Who says Home Ec's useless?" she said, grinning at him. Kyle felt uncomfortable. Even in this place, there was something really disturbing about the girl. Something particularly dangerous.

"Where to tonight, Fearless Leader?" Shadow asked Janice.

"It's Friday," Janice replied. "Where do you think?"

"Electric Avenue!" Smoke replied. She was already pulling on her heavy black cloak.

"We're going out for a while," Janice said, turning to Kyle. "You can hang out here if you want."

"I want to come along."

Shadow and Smoke just laughed. "This may be a little too intense for you, schoolboy," Smoke said.

"Maybe you should just stay inside where it's safe," Shadow added.

"You kind of stand out," Janice said, looking him up and down. He towered over her and the others. Even in old clothes, Kyle knew there was still something about him that screamed suburbia.

"I want to go with you," he said, determined.

Janice looked at him, then at the others. She shrugged. "Whatever."

"Find him something else to wear," Janice said. "So he doesn't embarrass us too much."

There were some protests, neither Smoke nor Shadow wanting him along. Janice quickly silenced them. She was still head of the family.

***

"Get your hands off me!" the man yelled as two large men in cowboy outfits led him quickly out of the bar. Once they were through the big main doors and out of sight of the rest of the clientele, they threw him roughly onto the sidewalk. He fell, sliding on the fresh snow, tearing a hole in the pants of his expensive suit. He stood up slowly, swearing at the two men. They were still grinning down at him, arms folded, obviously enjoying this part of their job. On his feet at last, he began to walk unsteadily to the row of parked cars along 11th Avenue, known as Electric Avenue because of its blocks of brightly lit clubs and bars. The two bouncers walked back inside, seeing their charge was on his way. The man leaned drunkenly against his

BMW as he fumbled in his coat pocket for the keys. He dropped them twice in the snow.

"That's the one," Janice said.

Quickly, the four of them swarmed from the shadows of the alley across the street. Kyle hung back a little, not yet ready to be anything other than an observer. He wore an old army coat, dyed black and smelling like something had died in the shredded lining. He watched as Smoke walked up to the man while the other two circled behind. This close, he saw that the drunk was about his father's age, dressed in a very expensive outfit. Janice knew how to pick her targets.

"Hey, mister," Smoke said, walking slowly up to him. "Can you give me a ride?"

The drunk looked over at her, puzzled, then grinning when he saw it was a young girl.

"What are you doing out this late?" the man said. "Isn't it past your bedtime?"

"Not yet," Smoke replied, slipping very close to him. The drunk looked down at her, still grinning. To Kyle, she appeared odd beside the older man, her black clothes and hair looking even more like a costume.

"Hey, darling," he said, about to put his arm around her shoulder, "didn't anyone tell you Halloween's over?" Just as his arm was about to rest on her shoulder, Smoke ducked, and pushed. The drunken man lost his balance and fell backwards on the hood of his car. Quickly, Janice and Shadow rushed forward, pulling him to his knees, pinning him to the ground. The man swore and struggled

101

as the three scrambled to get his wallet. Kyle stood nearby, not knowing what to do.

Smoke stood up, grinning, holding the wallet and something else while Shadow and Janice continued to hold down the struggling man.

"Look what I got!" she yelled out. Smoke held out a set of car keys, shaking them. "Let's go for a ride!"

"No!" Janice said. "We just want the money!"

"Why not?" Smoke shouted. "It's been ages since we boosted a car this nice!"

The man had stopped struggling, exhausted. But when he heard Smoke threatening to steal his car, he seemed to find his strength again. He screamed and swore and, unbelievably to Kyle, stood up, tossing Janice and Shadow away from him.

"Punks!" he screamed, lurching at Smoke. "No one's stealing my car!"

Smoke was startled and began to step back, ducking as the man grabbed for her. Shadow was on his feet again and grabbed the man by the neck. With all his strength, the man elbowed Shadow aside, and he fell to the street, fumbling inside his coat for his knife. Smoke, seeing the man attack Shadow, yelled and jumped on his back, the car keys tossed away, forgotten. The man swung her around, easily tossing her off. She bounced hard against the side panels of a parked van.

"Stop!" Janice screamed. "Let's get out of here!"

Kyle saw that a few people had begun to gather around. The drunken man was struggling to grab at Shadow who was still on the ground, scrabbling backwards to keep clear of him. Kyle was worried. Shadow's opponent was a full-grown man and Shadow, despite being street hardened, was still a boy. Janice was trying to get everything back under control when they heard Smoke scream in rage, and, pulling her long knife, rush the man.

Kyle acted quickly, not having time to think it through. He rushed forward, ducking down and tackling the drunk, just like he was a practice bag. The man flew over Kyle's shoulder and landed heavily on the pavement, winded. Still screaming and cursing the man, Smoke rushed forward, knife raised. Kyle grabbed her arm, holding her back inches from the drunk's throat.

"Let *go* of me!" She was struggling, trying to twist free.

"Move!" Janice yelled back, grabbing Smoke by the other arm. Shadow was on his feet again, looking embarrassed and bewildered.

"Damn punks," the drunk said, somehow getting to his feet again. He came at Kyle while Smoke still howled. Janice blocked her from slashing at the drunk.

"Let's get out of here!" Janice shouted. Kyle stood his ground as the drunken man rushed him, pushing him hard. He could smell the man's cologne, the alcohol on his breath. What am I doing, Kyle thought. Suddenly he began to see what was happening here, that this was a person, frightened and alone. It was no different than last night, when the punks attacked him. Kyle loosened his grip, about to let go, when the man swore and pushed him back. He aimed a punch at Kyle, which glanced painfully off his temple. Kyle's anger rushed back and he grabbed the man by the lapels of his expensive coat and slammed him hard against the van. He dragged him along the side, then slammed him hard against the next car, furious. The man had gone limp and Kyle looked into his eyes, saw the fear there.

"Kyle!" Janice shouted again. "Move! *Now*!"

Kyle turned around, heard the doors of the bar open, and saw the same two large bouncers appear, wondering what the commotion was. The others turned to see the bouncers rush down the stairs toward them. Kyle dropped the man, who then stayed on the ground, cowering between the parked cars. Smoke was still screaming, still wanting to get at him, as Kyle and Janice dragged her away. They ran back into the alley, trying to escape into the shadows, with the bouncers only a few steps behind. The four of them climbed fences and zigzagged through alleyways until Kyle was completely lost. Finally they emerged once more into another alley. They ran along until they reached a doorway guarded by two very large, bearded men. Kyle heard the muffled sound of music from behind the heavy loading dock doors. The two bearded men merely nodded and kept their ground while Smoke and Shadow slipped through the door. The blast of music was deafening for the split second it was open. Smoke looked back, then deliberately slammed the door in his face. Kyle hesitated and one of the men grabbed him by the arm, checking him over. He felt a moment of anxiety, not knowing what he had done to make this man suspicious. Kyle and the man stared at each other, neither looking away. There was another blast of sound as the door opened once more.

"It's okay," Janice said. "He's with me."

The large man still held on, his huge hand digging painfully into Kyle's upper arm. Finally, with a grunt, he let Kyle go. Janice smiled and held out her hand to him. Kyle took it gladly and followed her inside.

They entered into a wall of noise and shadows and Kyle saw he was in some kind of illegal after-hours place. The air was cold and smoke-filled, music blared from a band writhing on a makeshift stage. In the mosh pit, dozens of kids slammed into each other, pushing and shoving as much as they were dancing. The ceilings were high and some kids sat on the open rafters, alone or in couples, their upper bodies moving in rhythm. Shadow spun around and grabbed Kyle by the arm, their faces only inches apart. At first, Kyle tensed, thinking Shadow was angry, then he saw the huge grin on his face as he began to hop about in time to the blaring music.

"Wasn't that a rush?" he screamed into Kyle's face. He was still barely audible over the music. "Extreme!"

He let go of Kyle and danced about again, slamming into total strangers. Janice just watched him, smiling. Smoke stood against the wall, smoking and sulking.

"That was totally, totally awesome!" Shadow shouted again as he danced toward Kyle. He had to laugh. He knew exactly how Shadow felt. Kyle still felt the rush, the charge of adrenalin coursing through his blood. It had all happened so fast. The robbery, the victim's unexpected counterattack, his own decision to step in. The chase.

"You did good back there," Janice yelled in his ear. "You stood with us." She handed him a warm beer and took a long swallow of her own. Kyle gulped it down, barely tasting it. She stared up at him, her pale blue eyes piercing him. Kyle felt a surge of emotion. He had felt this way only a few times before. When he was young, and his father praised him — a rare occurrence. Or when he had played well and basked in the cheers of his coach and teammates. He felt as though he had passed some rite of initiation.

"Only next time," she said, "listen to me when I say go!" She looked over at Smoke, who was still sulking and glaring at Kyle. "You too!"

"Just tell schoolboy if he ever grabs me again, I'll come after him!"

Kyle looked back at her, trying to imitate the same bored expression he had seen so many times before. Smoke walked quickly away, looking for something to drink. She ignored Shadow's pleas to dance with him. Kyle felt that some invisible door had opened and he had been allowed inside. He had walked these streets for weeks, and now, for the first time, he no longer felt like an outsider. He leaned back against the peeling wall, feeling the cold seep into his shoulders but he didn't care. He sipped his beer slowly and looked out at the crowd writhing and stomping in the smoke and shadows of the crowded room. He glanced up at the high ceiling again. A girl stood on a rafter, leaning casually against a support beam. Her pose was identical to his own and he knew she was mimicking him, though he could barely see her through the smoky haze. He could make out that she was thin and tall, with a spiked shock of short greenish hair. He couldn't see her eyes, but he was certain she was staring at him. There was something familiar about her. He pushed himself away from the wall, wanting to get a better look.

"Hey!" Kyle looked to his right, startled by a shout in his ear. Janice was grinning up at him. When she smiled, Kyle noticed, her whole appearance changed. It made her a different person.

"I wanna *move!*" she yelled and took hold of his hand, leading him into the crowd. He glanced back up at the rafters, but the girl was gone.

"Dance!" Janice screamed as Kyle stood still while the sea of kids surged around him. Slowly, Kyle began to move in rhythm to the music. He looked down at her, seeing the grin on her usually calm face. The light made her eyes seem even bluer and there was a flush of pink under her pale skin. Kyle smiled back and moved closer to her. He danced with Janice and Shadow in the crowd of yellow, green, and purple hair, of pierced flesh and leather and jangling metal chains, and felt the adrenalin surge again and knew he belonged here. Janice bumped up against him, her black cloak thrown off, gyrating to the music, staring directly into his eyes, inviting him to move with her. He danced, losing himself in the music. For perhaps the first time in his life Kyle didn't worry about what he should be doing or how he should behave. He just wanted to be here now, with Janice.

# Chapter 13

Kyle stared across the rooftops at the flame burning on top of the Calgary Tower. The clouds were low again, and the orange glow of city lights reflected off them, rolling around in the early morning stillness. He had no idea what time it was, but he sensed that dawn wasn't far away.

"That flame's really something," Kyle said to Janice. They both sat on old blankets near an open grate of a small cubbyhole; Kyle had no idea what it had been before. He guessed it might have been a place where security people could check the levels below. Here, heat still blasted; this part of the abandoned parkade was still attached to the neighbouring office tower. Steam blew from the grate, pouring up and over the edge of the parkade roof. "It must be three or four metres high. Imagine the heat that thing's giving off."

"Yeah," Janice said softly. "Too bad it's too far away to do anyone any good."

After two or three hours dancing and drinking at the illegal club, the four kids had stumbled home, still laughing and telling stories of the evening's adventures. Even Smoke had relaxed, although not enough to completely forgive Kyle. He had smiled, noticing how their exploits were exaggerated when finally relayed to others in the gang not fortunate enough to be eyewitnesses. Neither of them able to sleep, Janice had invited Kyle to join her on the roof. He felt flattered and excited at an opportunity to be alone with her.

"Can I sit beside you?" he asked a little sheepishly. He had stopped looking up at the Tower. She shrugged, not looking at him, just staring off into the night. He moved close beside her, as close as he dared. His arm brushed gently against hers. He found the touch exciting, despite the layers of clothes they wore. He glanced at her as she stared out, lost in her own world. He wondered what she was thinking about so intensely. And he wondered why he felt so attracted to her.

It was true she was much too thin, too pale, not particularly clean. But there was something there, a definite attraction that he couldn't define. The girls he had dated in the past were the complete opposite of Janice. Bubbly, blonde, and healthy. He had never felt any need to hold intimate conversations with any of them. And he knew they felt the same. He had never met anyone as strong, or as independent as Janice before.

"It's kind of tight in here, isn't it?" Kyle said, looking around at the small cubbyhole. He knew he was babbling, but couldn't help it. Janice was too quiet. "Don't you feel a little trapped?"

"I don't go anywhere before checking all my exits. It's the only way to survive," she said. Kyle paused again. Another conversation-killing reply.

"I love the Christmas lights they have here," he said, trying once more. "I guess it's not cool or anything, but I've always liked Christmas." He looked over at her, but she still stared off, not responding. He felt a need to open up to her, to make her understand what he was really like. This change in her mood from earlier in the evening was disorienting.

"When I was a kid," he said, a little embarrassed at the memory, "I used to get this weird, funny kind of feeling at Christmas."

"Me too," Janice said, not looking up. "When I got older I realized it was just a head cold."

That shut him up for a while. He couldn't think of any more conversation-starters. They both stared out at the silent city for a while, and Kyle saw that the sun was beginning to rise. Soon, the streets below would be filled with cars. He thought desperately of something to say, something that would break her silence. He was deeply confused. Usually, when girls took him somewhere to be alone, they were a lot less hostile than Janice. He saw a small black object sticking out from the folds of her coat. Quickly, he reached out and grabbed it. It was a small, black notebook, shut with a rusty metal clasp.

"So what's this?" he said, jokingly. "You keeping a diary too?"

"Yeah," Janice said. "Something like that. Now give it back." She reached out for it but Kyle was glad to finally get a reaction from her. He pulled it back, farther from her reach. His hand hit the low ceiling of the cubbyhole and something slipped out of the book. It fluttered slowly and Kyle grabbed it in mid-air. It was a folded newspaper clipping, old and yellowed. Kyle began to open it, seeing only the headline. "Three Dead in Grisly Accident." There was a subhead, something about a young girl being the lone survivor. It was all he was able to read before Janice grabbed for it.

"Give me that back!" she screamed. Stunned by her reaction, he let her tear both the clipping and the book from his hands. She got up on her knees and scrabbled as far away from him as the tiny space would allow.

"Sorry," he said. "I was just playing around."

Janice didn't answer right away. She knelt there in the cold, staring out through the glass, cradling her book, the clipping once more safely tucked inside.

"Was that you?' Kyle asked. "Was that your family in the article?"

Janice continued to stare ahead, cradling the book. She sat silently for what seemed like minutes.

"What do you want to hear?" she said softly. "Life sucks. Even you've figured that one out by now."

Kyle was getting angry. All night at the dance she had been close to him, touching him. Something had happened between them. He was sure of it when she invited him up here. But now, since they had been alone, she had been cold. He had had about enough of her attitude.

"I don't need this!" Kyle said. "I'm sorry I happened to have been luckier than you and your pals! I'm sorry I didn't have the great opportunity to live on the streets or be as cool as you! If you thought I was such a loser then why did you invite me up here?"

Kyle got up on his knees and began to crawl toward the exit.

"Wait," Janice said. "I'm sorry. I get … weird sometimes."

She looked up at him and smiled. Kyle knew she knew what she looked like, her dark make-up, the pale skin, the teardrop tattoo; they both understood she was making fun of herself. Kyle still felt he should leave, but something made him want to stay with her.

"I guess I shouldn't have touched your diary," he said, trying to smooth things over.

"It's not a diary," she said softly. "They're poems."

"Really?" Kyle said, sounding more excited than he was about poetry. "Stuff you wrote?"

She nodded.

"Would you let me read them sometime?"

"You don't look like the poetry type," she said, smiling at him again. Once more, he noticed how her smile transformed her. Kyle adjusted his position on the blankets and huddled a little closer to the warm air blasting from the grate. The cold seemed to have no visible effect on Janice.

He just shrugged. "I'd be interested in yours," he replied.

"We'll see," she said. "I don't know if I like you that much." She turned to face him and must have seen the puzzled look on his face. She came over and sat cross-legged on the blankets, facing him, but still keeping her distance.

"I've been on the street since I was eight, since the accident. Maybe a few months off here and there at some foster home or detention hall or something. I haven't kept a lot to myself over the years. A girl on the street ... everyone thinks they can take anything they want from her. All I have that's still mine are my poems. I don't share them with just anyone."

Kyle nodded, not understanding completely, but respecting what she said. He leaned forward and put a hand on her cheek. Her skin felt cold.

"You must like me a little," he said. "Or you wouldn't have wanted to bring me up here."

She gently took his hand away, held it while she looked at him.

"Look, I'm sorry. It was wrong," she said. "We're too different."

Kyle leaned back again, feeling his face flush slightly. He was about to reply when he heard a creak and spun around, half expecting to see someone attack. Something about being here on the street had made him paranoid. Stash, the silent little girl, emerged through the trap door, and looked over at them.

"What's the matter, Bud?" Janice asked. "Couldn't sleep?" Stash nodded and crawled toward her. Janice

114

opened her arms and the little girl snuggled up to her. It was a scene Kyle had enacted with his mother countless times when he was a child. Janice led Stash back to the warmth of the grate, wrapping them both up in the filthy blankets. She began to hum softly in a pleasant, clear voice. Stash stared at Kyle as Janice rocked her. Then, surprisingly, she got up and crawled over to him. She snuggled up to him just as she had to Janice. He looked down at her, then back at Janice, who was clearly just as stunned by the little girl's actions. At first, he just sat there, not knowing what to do. Janice wrapped her arms around herself, nodding at Stash. It took a second or two, but Kyle finally caught on. He hugged the tiny girl and felt her snuggle even closer to him.

"I've never seen her do that before," Janice said quietly. She looked up at Kyle and he just shrugged, as bewildered as she was.

Soon, despite the cold, Stash was asleep, rocked in Kyle's arms. He watched as Janice stroked the girl's hair.

"How did she end up on the street?" he asked.

"I took her," Janice said. "We were in a foster home together. I figured it was better than what they were doing to her there." Kyle said nothing, just watched the sleeping girl and tried not to think of what she'd seen in her short life.

"That really is some birthmark she has," Kyle said, trying to change the course of the conversation once more.

"Birthmark?" Janice said, looking up at him. "You think that's what it is?

She shook her head and looked down at the girl. "When she was about two or three, she was still living with her mother. I guess she had a cold or something. Her nose had been running for days. Apparently, this really upset her mother. Seemed wiping her little girl's nose cut too much into her drinking time or whatever. She decided to fix it once and for all. She poured lighter fluid in her nose and lit it."

"Oh God!" Kyle said. He felt a sick feeling in his stomach. He looked away, not wanting Janice to see how much the story had upset him.

"I remember something you said earlier," Janice said softly, but Kyle could feel the bitterness in her words. "You wondered why we were so calm about Meghan disappearing. Let me tell you something. Stash, Smoke, Shadow, all of the others, they're my family now. You think what happened to Stash is sick? Compared to some of us, she got off easy."

She leaned back against the wall staring at him as he rocked Stash, still sleeping soundly.

"Every single one of us is here because we have to be — not by choice. This isn't some game! None of us have a nice warm bed and supper waiting for us at home when we get tired of playing street kid."

"What are you talking about?" Kyle asked. He knew exactly what she meant, and he felt his temper rise again. "You know what happened! You know as well as I do that Meghan can't go home!"

"Oh really?" Janice replied scornfully. "You really think Age would go after her back in the burbs? Grow up! Both of you! They're finished with her. There's plenty more stupid girls out there! They couldn't care less about the one that got away!

"Meghan can go home anytime she wants. But she likes the game too much. When I decided to help her, I got my kids, my family, mixed up in someone else's fight. Your sister's not who I'm worried about now."

"It can't be that bad," Kyle replied. "And anyway, how's he going to find out you helped her?"

"You've been out here what? A few school nights? A few weekends up past your bedtime? You think that makes you some kind of expert? Word travels fast down here. And like I told you before, the only thing that matters is your reputation! You think Age is going to let people know that a bunch of punk kids screwed up his plans? He spent money on recruiting Meghan. If she had gone home, he would have just written it off. The price of business. But I got involved in his business. I screwed up his plans, not Meghan. And that's something totally different."

She looked at him for what seemed like minutes. Kyle was shocked. And ashamed. She was partly right, he had been enjoying the game. So had Meghan until things had gone wrong. He wasn't totally convinced that Meghan could just go home after all that had happened. But now he began to see for the first time how much danger she had brought to Janice and the others.

"I can help you. We can find someplace to hide."

"For how long? A week? A month? The street's a small world. He'll find us."

"Maybe he'll just give up."

Janice laughed and looked down at Stash. "Not this time. We've pulled this stunt on him too many times."

"How many?" Kyle asked.

"Starting with me?" Janice replied, then shrugged. "How many kids you see down there tonight?"

"Including Stash?"

"Especially Stash," Janice said. Kyle looked down and began gently rocking the girl again. He saw the girl wasn't sleeping. Her eyes were open and she was studying him silently.

# Chapter 14

Kyle wandered the streets all the next day. He had called home, knowing his mother would be working, and left a message on the machine, telling her he would be home soon. Downtown Saturday was unusually busy, the Christmas shoppers getting a head start. Everywhere he walked he saw street kids. They were easily recognizable to him now, distinct from the other ragged kids just hanging out. He saw the hard look in their eyes, the pale features, the ever-present knapsacks carrying all of their worldly possessions. In a doorway next to a hamburger joint on 7th Avenue he saw three girls panhandling; one of them played with a fat, grey squirrel, stroking its thick fur. Kyle was fascinated by the sight of the squirrel, obviously a pet, running up and down the girl's shoulders, taking the crumbs she offered as she gently kissed its head. He moved on quickly when the girls started to notice him stare.

Late in the afternoon, in the Devonian Gardens, Kyle had the sensation he was being watched. He tried to ignore it at first, but the feeling was strong. As casually as he could, he stood up and walked up the tiered walkway. To his right, he caught a glimpse of greenish hair. A girl was sitting cross-legged high above him, noisily sipping a drink through a twisted, plastic straw. She wore a thick green overcoat — army surplus — and stared down at him just as she had done last night. Once more her face was in shadow, and the heavy make-up she wore helped disguise her features. Just like last evening, Kyle felt he knew her.

He stood and called to her, "What do you want?"

She stared silently down at him, still sucking on the straw, then nodded to Kyle's right. He glanced over his shoulder and saw two security guards walking deliberately toward him. He guessed he must have overstayed his welcome, like other teens he had seen being kicked out his first time here. When he looked back up, the girl was gone. He started to run up the stairs, zigzagging through the terraced benches. The guards were yelling behind him, ordering him to stop.

Kyle burst through the doors that led back into the shopping centre. The girl was nowhere in sight. He pushed himself through the shoppers, looking frantically for her. There were too many levels, too many exits — he knew it was hopeless finding her unless she wanted to be found. Frustrated, Kyle sat heavily on a bench, the festive music ringing in his ears. It was crazy, but welling up in him was the feeling that he knew who the green-haired girl was. He just didn't know why she was playing this game with him. He looked up, through the high glass windows of the mall, past the giant Christmas wreath that hung there. It was getting dark and he knew where he had to be.

*** 

Kyle woke with a start. For a moment, he felt disoriented, then he recognized the smell of burning wax and the other, less pleasant smell of the blankets he had crawled into. He had no idea what time it was, but the fire in the centre pit had died down a little. Only a few of the other, younger kids were left in the hideout. He could hear their soft breathing as they slept. Stash lay asleep beside him, curled up in a ball. He pulled the covers over her and stood up as gently as he could.

He threw more wood on the fire until it caught again, immediately taking some of the chill away. Kyle guessed the others had taken off for their nightly "business" rounds. Exhausted from the sleepless night before, Kyle had fallen asleep while they were drinking and building up the courage to go out.

He stretched and rubbed his back to get the kinks out, then reached into the battered fridge for something to drink. Bundled up against the cold, he decided to go upstairs to Janice's hiding space and stare at the city lights until she returned. He had nearly made it to the top floor of the parkade when he heard a sound. Startled, he turned quickly but saw no one there. He waited, listening, moving quietly into the shadows, trying to be less of a target. When he heard nothing else, he grinned at his own panic and stepped out of the shadows once more. This high up, some of the windows hadn't been boarded up and he could see the streets below. Standing there, looking out, he barely noticed the two vans that pulled silently up to the curb, lights off.

The wind had begun to pick up again, blowing through the shattered windows and Kyle shivered. He caught a glimpse of movement at the corner of his eye and turned slowly toward it, a little less apprehensive now, assuming Janice or one of the others had returned. A short distance away, someone stood in the shadows, leaning against a pillar. Kyle leaned forward, squinting, trying to see who it was. The figure moved toward him silently, and he began to make out features. Immediately he saw it wasn't one of Janice's family. Even in the gloom, Kyle could make out the bright clothes under the old army surplus coat and the greenish hair. The figure stopped less than three metres away and he waited, letting her make the first move. He didn't have to wait long.

"Hello, Big Brother," Meghan said.

Kyle stood perfectly still, a rush of confused emotions pouring through him. He wasn't sure exactly how he felt seeing Meghan standing there in front of him at last. Never before in his life had he felt so overwhelmed, so overjoyed at seeing someone. He wanted to rush over to her to hug her! But he wanted to make sure that he wasn't mistaken again ... he couldn't quite believe the skinny punker who stood in front of him was actually Meghan. Then she began to laugh and he had no doubt.

"I've seen you look pretty dumb sometimes, Big Brother, but nothing like this!"

Kyle could only imagine how he must look to her, standing there, motionless, his mouth gaping open. He began to grin at her remark.

"At least you've discovered a sense of humour since I've been gone," she said, seeing his grin. "And look at you. Where's the baby face? You almost look like a man now." She began to circle him slowly. Kyle took a step toward her and she stepped back quickly, as if he had made some threatening move.

"Whoa! Just take it easy, Kyle! I'm just here to talk!" Meghan held a hand out, a warning to keep his distance. She kept circling around, staying just out of reach.

"Meghan," he said, at last finding his voice. "I can't believe it. I can't believe you're here!" Even as he spoke them, Kyle knew his words sounded trite, hopelessly inadequate. Meghan just circled around him, quickly ducking behind posts, reappearing just as quickly. He thought he saw her smile in the dim light spilling through the cracked and filthy windows.

"I guess I'm glad to see you, too, Big Brother," she said. "Who'd've thunk it!"

Kyle still felt the need to grab her, to see her up close. She kept dancing around him, fidgeting, occasionally looking over her shoulder. It irritated him.

"Could you stop and just talk to me?" he said, immediately fearing that he had spoken too harshly.

"Can't do that, Big Brother," Meghan said. "Gotta keep moving. You've been around long enough to know that."

"There's no one else here."

"Habit," she replied, shrugging. Kyle saw that when she spoke, she nervously raked her fingers through her closely cropped hair. He guessed it was another habit she had picked up. Her eyes were wide and glassy.

"I've been looking for you for weeks. Trying to get you to come home."

"Where's home? That little shack in the Northeast?" She slowed down slightly, standing in better light. He saw that she wore layers of tight T-shirts under her ripped overcoat. Her stomach was bare and he saw that she now had a pierced navel and was terribly, terribly thin.

"I don't think so," she continued. "Besides. Too much has happened."

Meghan hopped up onto the low concrete railing that edged the down ramp. She walked slowly along it, arms wide, balancing like a tightrope walker. The athlete in Kyle noticed how graceful she was as she teetered on the edge. If she slipped, she would tumble to the next level, easily a four-metre drop. He was too far way to help if she lost her balance. He held his breath and frantically thought of what to say next.

"If you're talking about Age, we can handle him. And anyway, Janice figures he'll leave you alone now. You could come home any time!"

Meghan stopped for a moment, to turn and face her brother. "Not even Janice knows it all."

"You must want to come home. You could've taken off to Vancouver when you had the chance!"

Meghan laughed and jumped off the railing back onto the concrete floor. Kyle was relieved.

"Those guys Janice set me up with figured I had to pay my way out. The trip wasn't worth what they were asking."

Kyle paused a moment, taking it in. "Why didn't you tell Janice that?"

"What for?" Meghan replied. "She probably knew what those guys'd want me to do. Nobody gets anything for free on the street."

"Janice helped you for free."

Meghan paused for a second and looked over at Kyle. She seemed to be considering this last statement.

"I guess that's why I'm here. I owe her."

Kyle stepped closer to her. This time she didn't step back, but she began to circle around him again. In the distance, he heard the faint sound of sirens. Meghan seemed to hear it as well. She grinned.

"What do you mean?" Kyle asked. She circled him still, but less than a metre away now. He could see her face clearly. It was thin, the high cheekbones pronounced. She wore heavy make-up, her eyes barely visible beneath a racoonlike application of mascara.

"Sorry to disappoint you, Big Brother. I didn't come here for a family reunion. I'm here to help Janice."

The wail of sirens was louder now. Kyle couldn't tell if they were police or fire trucks.

"I've been snooping around, looking for another way out. I accidentally heard that Age and the boys decided to teach Janice a lesson tonight," Meghan said, walking over to the windows. She nodded toward Kyle, indicating the street below. Kyle walked over and looked down. He saw the vans still idling below. For the first time he wondered what they were doing there. Then it hit him. He looked over at Meghan.

"I see it's all coming together now," she said gently, watching his face. She stood on the other side of the window, still at last. "I called the cops before I came up here. Told them there was a big gang fight happening."

She stepped back now and for a moment, Kyle saw the old Meghan under the mask. Saw his little sister the way she was only a few months before. She moved and it was gone, a trick of the light.

"I wasn't planning on being here when they arrived. But I didn't plan on seeing you at the club last night."

"Come home with me, Meghan," Kyle said at last. "Please."

"I don't think I ever heard you say that before, Big Brother," she said. She shook her head and began to walk away, back into the shadows. The sirens were only blocks away now. "You shouldn't be here either."

"Wait!" he shouted, and scrambled around reaching in his back pocket. "Here," he said, handing a wad of folded bills to her. She hesitated, then took the money from him, her fingers brushing his for an instant.

"Quite a pile," she said. "Dad still sending you those cheques?"

"You knew about that?"

Meghan laughed again. "Of course! Both me and Mom knew. You and Dad have your good points, I guess. But neither of you are exactly subtle."

"He never gave you anything?"

"Me? I'm just a dumb girl. I'd just spend it on frivolous things. Besides, I'm supposed to wait for the right guy to come along to take care of me. Just like Mom did."

Kyle knew exactly what she meant. He recognized their father's beliefs instantly.

"He's in town now. Looking for you."

Meghan paused for an instant. "Really? Isn't that something."

Red and blue lights flashed through the windows as the police cars finally appeared along 9th Avenue. The sound of sirens was deafening, and through the window, Kyle saw the vans below begin to pull away, just as the police turned the corner. There were three police cars — two followed the vans, the other pulled up on the curb. Kyle turned back to grab Meghan, to get her out of here.

She was gone. Kyle shouted her name, knowing that he'd never be heard over the sirens. He ran, knowing he had to go up to get away. He prayed

127

that Meghan had gone up too. He ran up the ramp, hearing the sirens, the shouts of police. On the walkway level, he ran into Janice's family as they pushed and shoved their way out, trying to escape. They must have returned only moments before, now they were scrambling for the exits again. For the first time, they looked less like a gothic street gang than a pack of frightened kids.

As they ran across the covered tunnel that led to the office building next door, Kyle looked down at the confused mass of cars and people below. Two more police cars had arrived. Alarms rang as the doors to the office building next door were kicked open. Kyle felt his heart pound as he ran down the stairs with the others still pushing and shoving, still swearing at each other. As they burst through the doors at street level and into the deserted back alley, the feeling of relief was overwhelming. The shouts and curses turned to laughter as the small gang ran along the alley, away from the sirens. As they emerged onto 8th Avenue, Kyle looked around, searching for Janice. He couldn't see her. He turned back as Smoke tried to rush past him. He grabbed her. Smoke swore at him to let go.

"Where's Janice?" he shouted.

"How should I know?" She continued her struggle to get free, but Kyle held her tightly.

"Where's everyone going now?"

"Like I'd tell you!" Smoke glared up at him. The look of pure hate she gave him made his blood run cold. He let her go. She swore once more and pushed him hard. Then she turned to run, joining the others as they ran wildly, whooping and laughing down the deserted avenue toward city hall. Kyle stood in the cold wind as the sun crept farther down the side of the glass-lined skyscrapers and felt totally alone.

# Chapter 15

Kyle sat across the tiny kitchen table from his father. Even in a casual golf shirt and khaki pants, his father seemed to personify wealth and authority. It was something Kyle had always admired about his father, something he himself had tried to emulate. These days, after the painful divorce, after the way he treated his mother and Meghan, the image was the only thing Kyle still admired.

His search for Meghan had opened his eyes in so many ways. He had begun to realize how lucky he had been. Growing up, he'd had the best clothes, gone to the best schools, lived with all the trappings of wealth. In the last months, he had begun to see that his life might not turn out the way he had always believed it would. Somehow, that didn't frighten him anymore.

His mother was bustling about in the other room, getting ready for an evening of work. Yet another realtor's Sunday. She had spent all day showing homes across the city and had many more hours ahead of her. For the first time, Kyle realized why his mother had been working so hard over the past weeks. Burying herself in her job was her way of coping with Meghan's disappearance. He also suspected that she was glad to be getting away from the cramped house and her ex-husband.

After sneaking out yet again, he was grounded. Again. He hadn't bothered to put up a fight this time. He knew how hard it would be to find either Meghan or Janice on the street if they didn't want to be found. He went back to school and football practice. Coach Kovacks was still allowing him to participate, even though he had already missed a game and several practices. They had had several meetings since that day when he and Paul had fought. So far, the coach was willing to cut him some slack. He wasn't sure about the rest of his team.

It had been over a week now since he had seen Meghan at the parkade. He had stayed home every night, hoping, waiting. He wasn't sure exactly who he wanted to hear more from, Meghan, or Janice.

Now father and son sat in silence, his father staring at nothing, busily preparing himself for the speech Kyle knew he was about to deliver to his wayward son. Kyle recognized the look.

Kyle glanced at his father, seeing his own face reflected there, older, more lined. It had always been easy to picture himself as an adult, the kind of man he was born to be. His father had made the picture perfectly clear.

Kyle looked away, thinking of that night with the gang. He thought of the well-dressed drunk, staggering to his expensive car. The image of the older man stopping to fondle the girl less than a third of his age sickened him. And Kyle had no trouble placing his own father in a similar situation.

"I have to talk to you," his father said at last. Kyle leaned back against the wall, waiting. "I don't quite know how to approach this," he said softly, putting his glass down on the table. Kyle smiled inwardly.

"I guess it's difficult for me since I haven't been around much …"

"That's funny," Kyle said, grinning, interrupting his father's well-rehearsed speech. He saw his father's face darken slightly, not expecting this. "That's the first time I really noticed how many times you use the word "*I*" to start a sentence."

"I'll try to watch that in the future," his father said, keeping the same careful tone.

"You just did it again," Kyle said, grinning.

"Very amusing," his father replied. His careful manner was becoming a bit more forced. "Can you forget the amateur psychology and let me continue?"

"Come on, Dad," Kyle said. "It's cute. I bet you never noticed you do it either."

"I'm trying to have a serious conversation here!" his father snapped. Kyle kept on grinning, ready for Bad Dad to emerge. He knew his father would hate the use of the word, cute, in describing his actions.

"You sound like your sister when you talk like this!"

"Yeah?" Kyle asked. "Do I really?" He stared at his father. "Good."

"What are you talking about now?"

"I'm talking about Meghan!" Kyle answered, his voice rising. "It would really bother you if your only son started acting as silly and irresponsible as your daughter! And," he continued, pausing for effect, just as he had learned from the master, "I'm talking about these!"

Kyle pulled a wad of paper from his shirt pocket and tossed them on the table between them. The cheques had been torn in pieces, but were still recognizable. His father saw immediately what they were and glared across at his son. Then he quickly glanced behind him to make sure Kyle's mother was still in the bathroom.

"How many?" his father asked softly, so far maintaining his temper.

"About three months' worth."

"I thought I taught you better than this," his father said.

"You did, Dad," Kyle replied. "Fortunately, in the last few months I started listening to a better teacher."

"That money was a pact between us. Something I expected you to understand. To honour."

"Honour, Dad? I must have missed that part of the lesson."

"I'm not doing this for me! I know what it was like at your age, not having a penny. I worked hard so my kids wouldn't have to. I don't want my son to walk around like a bum, working at some lousy minimum-wage job!"

"Thanks, Dad. I finally figured out where I got that particular prejudice from. What about Meghan, huh, Dad?" Kyle asked. "Didn't she deserve the same pact? And what about Mom? You think she likes living like this?"

"That's different! You mother can take care of herself! She seems to enjoy showing everyone she can make it on her own. And Meghan's still too young. What would she do with the money?"

"Maybe it wasn't just the money, Dad," Kyle said as he stood up. He had been ready for a fight. Ready to show his father that he had figured him out, saw through his little games. But there was no joy in it, arguing with his father had become a pointless exercise. The fight was no longer in him. He no longer needed to prove anything to this man.

"Maybe you could have just once treated Meghan like she was a person. The funny thing is, Dad, between the two of us, Meghan is the most like you."

"Really? And how is that?"

"You know. Selfish. Stubborn. Only thinking of her own needs."

"I told you before!" his father shouted. "Don't try playing psychologist with me!"

"Can't you just once talk to him without yelling?"

Kyle's mother had appeared in the hallway, looking in. She looked at Kyle and then back at her ex-husband. Kyle saw his father's hand carefully cover the small pile of torn cheques, hiding them from her. It would be so easy to say something, to reveal their dirty little secret. He and his father looked away from each other, silent. Kyle stood up, wanting to get away. The silence between the three of them was suffocating. When the phone rang in the next room, his mother started.

"I'll get it," Kyle said, pushing past his mother in the narrow hall. He was glad of the excuse to get away from his parents. He picked up the receiver, expecting it to be one of his mother's real estate clients.

"Hello?"

"Hey, tough guy! Did I disturb your beauty sleep?"

The voice was unmistakable. Kyle felt his heart begin to beat harder, just as it had done last weekend. He sat down heavily on the sofa, trying to compose his thoughts. He had a second chance and he wanted to make the best of it.

"Don't say my name, Big Brother. This is between you and me. Act like I'm an old pal or something."

"Okay," Kyle said weakly. He desperately wanted to play along.

"Is the whole family gathered once again?"

"Yeah, that's right," Kyle answered.

"In the room with you?"

"No. In the kitchen."

"That must be something. The two of them in the same room without lawyers present."

"It's something all right," Kyle said. He leaned back on the couch, twisting around to look out the front window, to make it harder for his parents to hear him. He had no idea why he felt he should keep Meghan's resurfacing from them, but he followed his instincts.

"How are they holding up?" Meghan asked softly. To Kyle it seemed almost an afterthought.

"Not good," Kyle said. He paused. "I want you to come home."

"I can't."

"We both know why you're staying out there. Don't you think you've caused enough damage?"

"I haven't even started, Big Brother," she replied.

There was a longer pause this time. Kyle waited, knowing that Meghan would speak again when she was ready.

"It's not over with Janice," she said. "Age and the others are going to try again. Tonight. After the cops and stuff last week, they're really pissed."

"How do you know all this?" Kyle asked.

"I just know, all right?" Meghan replied, defensive. "Listen. I don't have a lot of time here. The other place Janice and the Goths squat is in the old Boyd building on 6th Avenue and 5th. You have to find Janice, tell them to stay away from there. You got it?"

"I got it! I just want to know how you know all this! How did you know that Age and the others were there last Friday?"

Kyle's voice was getting louder. He felt his frustration rise as the situation once more slipped away from him. He knew word got around on the streets, that Meghan could easily have overheard things. In the back of his mind, another, more sinister explanation for all this was beginning to form. He tried to fight it. He couldn't believe his sister was capable of doing what he had begun to suspect.

"Just do what I say!" Meghan continued. "Whatever happens, don't let them get caught there tonight."

"Why can't you warn her? You know the streets better than me!"

"Can't, Big Brother. I'll be a long way away." There was another pause. "Bye, Kyle. Maybe we'll run into each other some day."

The line went dead and Kyle put the phone down. He sat back heavily on the sofa, drawing up his knees and burying his head in his hands.

"Who was that?" his mother asked. Kyle jerked his head up, not aware she had come into the room. She was good at sneaking up on him this evening. "Was that something to do with Meghan?" Kyle felt his guilt grow. He didn't have time right now to explain things to his mother. He knew what kind of reaction she would have if he told her that he had found her, then let her go again. Right now, he had to get downtown, to find Janice and the others. To warn them.

"It was nothing, Mom," Kyle said, standing. It took every effort to control his emotions.

"Don't tell me it was nothing, Kyle!" she replied, grabbing his arm as he tried to get past her once more. "You look terrible! Who was on the phone?"

"Just a prank call. Someone who thinks he's funny." He pulled his arm away and headed back down the hall to the front door. Now both his parents followed him as he grabbed his winter coat.

"Where are you going?" his mother asked. "You're not going out of this house again!"

Kyle ignored her and reached for the door handle. His father moved in front of him, spinning him around until they were face to face. Even Kyle was impressed at how quickly his father could move.

"You heard your mother," he said. "You're not going anywhere!"

Kyle just looked at his father, at the hand clutching his jacket tightly.

"We can fix this," his father said. "But we have to do it together."

"We've never done anything together, Dad," Kyle said. "We've only ever done things your way."

"Okay," his father replied. "I get it. I'm a lousy father, okay? But I'm here to help. I want to help."

"You don't have a clue what's going on," Kyle replied.

"Let him go, Robert," Kyle's mother said.

"We can't just let him go back to the street!"

"Let him go!" she said. "I'm sick of you interfering in our lives! Let him go now!"

Stunned, his father stepped back. He seemed totally confused. Kyle straightened up and opened the door. With a final glance at his mother, he walked out.

Running down the sidewalk, fastening his jacket, he wondered who he was really angry with. He thought again of Meghan showing up so unexpectedly. He knew there was only one explanation, only one way she would have known that Age and the other bikers would be there, would know where Janice and the others were squatting.

Meghan had told them.

# Chapter 16

Kyle ran down 5th Avenue, head ducked, trying to minimize the cold wind that blew in his face. Freezing crystals of snow blasted him, forcing their way along his neck, burrowing past his collar and stinging his flesh. The wind was continuous, never seeming to slow down. As he ran past a burned-out home, he checked his watch. It was past nine.

He was angry with himself again. He had gone to the wrong 5th Avenue and 6th Street. Still unfamiliar with the city, he had arrived at the southwest corner, only to find block after block of modern office buildings. He had wasted valuable time before realizing Meghan had meant 5th and 6th *Southeast*. As he ran, desperately trying to make up lost time, Kyle once more blamed it on his own stupidity, his lack of mental agility. He wished yet again he had been born with a mind as quick as Meghan's. Or Janice's. A small voice tried to remind him that in many ways, this was still a largely unknown city, that he was allowed to make mistakes. Kyle ignored the voice and ran faster.

He knew how smart Janice was. She would have already known that it was Age and the others outside the old parkade last week. She would know that he would still be after them. Janice would find a safe place to hide out. If Meghan was right, her safe place was the most dangerous place she could be.

Fifth Avenue was still busy with cars and people out having a good time. As soon as he ran across Macleod Trail, into the southeast, the traffic nearly disappeared, the area immediately seedier. The sounds of the city seemed muffled, blanketed by the decay. He ran past abandoned buildings and old men and women, drunk, staggering in alleys. Young girls strolled along, looking bored and cold. They stood at sudden attention each time a car drove slowly past. Outside an old warehouse, a bonfire burned in the loading dock, surrounded by gnarled figures passing a bottle wrapped in brown paper. They called out to him as he passed. Kyle ran on, faster, slowing only once when he spotted a police car cruising slowly along the desolate street. He quickly ducked into a stairwell, not wanting to explain to the police what he was doing here. The car's headlights swept across the brick of the stairwell, just above Kyle. He turned his eyes away, momentarily blinded, and held his breath, sure that he had been spotted. The police car drove on, turning another corner. Kyle stood slowly, blinking, waiting for his night vision to return, hardly believing his luck. A little more confident, he walked out on the sidewalk, and began to trot. As the headlights had lit up the doorway, he had caught a glimpse of some graffiti, the same familiar one he had seen many times before.

"Age is the enemi," Kyle said softly as his trot turned into a full run.

He reached 6th at last and slowed down, holding a hand to the painful stitch in his side. As he trotted along the icy street, he saw the old building standing alone in a field of rubble and garbage. It was at least ten storeys high, an old red-brick warehouse, typical of the kind built near the turn of the century. The ragged windows were covered in rusted wire mesh, the sealed wooden doors of the loading dock faced an abandoned railway track. Near the top of the building he heard the sound of pigeons cooing and saw the words "Boyd Building," painted white on black, faded by decades of neglect. He also saw smoke escaping from somewhere inside, torn quickly away in the cold wind.

Kyle's breathing was back under control as he climbed over a discarded dumpster, ducking easily under a wire fence that had once kept the public away from the abandoned building. Only tattered bits of rusted metal were left and he easily slipped through. He saw no vans waiting on the streets with engines running, as he had last week. He allowed himself a moment of relief, believing he was here in time. Kyle jumped down from the dumpster, nearly wrenching an ankle on the broken bricks that lay partially hidden beneath the thin layer of snow and ice. As he crept closer to the building, his heart his heart began to pound. The north side of the building gave him some cover as he crept along, looking for an entrance. Like the parkade, he expected to find some hidden way in, one only Janice and her gang would know. He worked his way along the building, checking the west, then the south side, but found nothing. A little uneasy, he had only one option left and crouched low as he headed toward the front on the east side, facing 6th Street. As he'd hoped, the street was completely deserted. The white glow of a single streetlight lit the facade of the building, and Kyle saw a wide brick staircase that led up to the high doors of the main entrance. Still wary, Kyle kept low in the shadow offered by the staircase.

In the distance he heard an ambulance or firetruck, the bells of a railroad crossing as a train passed an intersection. Nothing else, no sounds from the building itself. At the front of the stairwell, Kyle twisted around to see the stairs and the entrance to the building. The doors were nearly 15-feet high, and had once been expensive and ornate. Now they were covered in buckled pieces of plywood, rotting and nailed tight. Perhaps not completely tight. On the far right, he saw that the bottom board was loose. The snow on the stairwell beneath it was trampled, and he saw other footprints on the stairs themselves. Lots of them. As he walked up slowly, it seemed to him that someone had kicked snow against the plywood boards in an effort to hide the marks made by dragging the board away from the doorway. Kyle knew that only someone leaving the building would have been able to attempt the cover-up.

Kyle took a deep breath, then pulled back the heavy plywood and squeezed himself through.

Inside, as the wood creaked back into place, he reached deep into the inside pocket of his jacket and pulled out his old camping flashlight. Unlike his visit to the parkade, this time he had come prepared. Kyle waited for a moment, listening. He thought he heard a faint thumping sound, coming from somewhere high above. It was too faint to be certain, but he thought it was music. He allowed himself a small smile. Music was a good sign. Music meant people and parties and fun.

He snapped on the flashlight and waved it around, and the room revealed itself in small circles of yellow light. The ceiling was high and domed, there were pillars that reached up into archways and the floor had once been covered in expensive marble. Now nearly all the marble was gone, leaving sharp, jagged patches of tarred concrete. Shuffling carefully along, Kyle passed by the boarded-up elevators to a thick wooden door inset with frosted glass. Miraculously, the glass was intact and the word *Stairs* was stencilled there in tall, black letters. The door swung open easily and Kyle began to climb up. Like the parkade, there was the dusty stench of decay and filth as he climbed. He saw old bits of tattered clothing, fast-food wrappers and discarded needles. He stepped carefully, his breath sometimes obscuring his way in the frigid air.

As he climbed, he heard the thumping sounds more distinctly, and he knew now it was music. He began to climb faster, hopeful once more. Now all he had to do was warn them, get them out of here before Age and his gang arrived.

He was slightly winded as he reached the 10th and last floor, the music loud and undeniable now. Still a little wary about sneaking up on the gang, Kyle carefully opened the door and stepped into the hall. On either side of him were rows of doors, most of them sealed shut. Furniture, old office desks and chairs lined the hall and Kyle had to be careful navigating through the mess. At the end of the hall was a large metal door. He had seen doors like it only in old movies. It was as wide as the hall and reached up to the ceiling. The two parts met horizontally in the centre, about four feet up. Kyle grabbed the leather strap in the centre of the door and pulled down, the top flap slid up into the ceiling as the bottom part slid down. The big room beyond was bright, lit with dozens of candles. The smoke from a fire disappeared through the torn rooftop. The music was incredibly loud, even louder than in the old hiding place.

The scene was familiar in so many ways. Clothes hung around the fire on wire lines stretching between concrete pillars. He saw vague shapes surrounding the dying fire, propped up on old bits of furniture. They were huddled together, sinking low, as if not wanting to be seen. Kyle stood in the doorway, unable to move. Even with the last heat from the dying fire, it was still cold in the room. He took a step forward and stopped, hearing a short, painful moan over the roar of the music. It took a moment before Kyle realized he had made the sound. The kids scrambled painfully out of his way as he approached slowly. They cowered and hid themselves in the shadows. He could see they were battered and terribly frightened. None of them tried to stop him.

Kyle walked up to them and saw Shadow. His face was swollen and bloodied.

"What happened?" he asked.

"Get out, before they come back," Shadow replied.

"They're gone," Kyle said, knowing he meant Age and his gang. Shadow didn't seem to believe him. He squatted down and wrapped his arms around his knees.

"Where's Janice?" Kyle asked.

Shadow lowered his head and shook it, not replying.

Kyle turned away from the pack of huddled, frightened kids. One step at a time, the flashlight hanging loosely at his side, he moved closer and closer to the fire. Kyle walked past the edge of the outer circle toward a dark figure lying partially covered in a pile of second-hand books. Her pale blue eyes were open and stared up at the ceiling. Two dark stains spread away from her black hair, mixing with the dust of the wooden floor, and Kyle found himself staring at her face, at the tiny teardrop tattooed under her right eye. He tried to breathe, tried to say something. No words came and instead he began to sink down, reaching out a hand, his flashlight dropping to the ground and rolling away under the books. Kyle leaned over Janice, hands shaking, unable to move any closer, unable to touch her.

He felt that he was slipping, that he had lost his balance as the music began to wind down, the batteries in the old blaster finally giving out. It took several seconds before the music died completely. In the empty silence he began to hear the moans, hear the crying. Still crouched over Janice, a movement caught his eye. In the space between two overturned desks he saw a tiny face, the strange red mark over her lip clearly visible. Stash was staring at Janice, oblivious to everything else. She sat with her knees up, arms wrapped around them, rocking back and forth, back and forth. As always, she was completely silent and Kyle carefully stepped over the books and the stained floor, toward her. As he neared, she seemed to see Kyle for the first time, looking intensely at him. She didn't seem frightened of him and made no move to get away as he reached out to her. Good, Kyle thought, she recognizes me. Then, only a foot or so away, she began to scream. It was the only sound he had ever heard from her. He reached out again and the screams were worse. He heard the moans and the sobbing around him intensify and he slipped and began to scrabble away from the terrible sound of Stash's screams. Tripping on the books and the slick, wet floor, Kyle somehow made it to his feet.

He ran.

He ran scrambling over the shapes in the darkness in the hall, tripping over the piled-up office furniture. He reached the stairs and descended down

146

into the stink and the blackness. More than once he tumbled, crashing head over heels, then dragged himself up again to run once more. Finally, near exhaustion, he made it to the ground floor. Stumbling in the near total darkness, feeling his way past the pillars, Kyle sensed rather than saw the entrance and slammed his full weight against the plywood. A vague memory of football practice surfaced before he heard a crack and fell outside as the wood gave, sending him sprawling on the snow-covered concrete stairs.

Kyle ran blindly through the streets, past the same people, the same buildings and desolation he had seen before. He ran until he was completely lost, until his legs no longer supported him and he collapsed in the snow. He pulled his knees to his chest and wound his arms around them tightly, and rocked back and forth, an unconscious imitation of Stash. He had no idea how long he lay there before the white police cruiser pulled slowly to a stop a few feet away and he saw the officers walk cautiously toward him. One of them crouched low, examining him. Through his shock and tears, Kyle saw the police officer was young, only a few years older than himself. He reached out and grabbing the policeman by the shoulder, Kyle saw that his hands had blood on them.

# Chapter 17

January 23

Dear Me,

Well, she was right. It does sound stupid. Dear Diary, Dear anything! But I guess that's the way you're supposed to do it. So here it is, the first entry in my very own diary. It may not be pretty, but it's just for me, right? I'm going to make damn sure no one ever sees this thing!

So, what should I talk about? Nothing much exciting really. I don't even know why I picked this particular day to start this. Well, maybe I do, but I'll get to that later.

I turned 18 yesterday. Big Day and all that stuff. I don't feel much like an adult, but I guess, officially, that's what I am. We had a cake and some presents and a party with some friends (I still have a couple it seems) at our place. Even Mom seemed to have a good time. I got a gift from Dad. It was in a small envelope. Wonder what that could possibly be? I burned it with my candles. You should have seen the look on Mom's face. I think she kind of enjoyed it, though.

I told everyone I was quitting the team. No big surprise since I've barely made practice in months. People asked me what I was going to do after I finish high school. Would I go to university? Travel? Maybe just bum around for a while? I really don't know myself. For the first time I really don't care what I do. I started volunteering at the Drop-In Centre after Christmas. Mom and I both did. So right now, that's my priority. No sign of Meghan, or Smoke or Shadow or anyone. It's like they all just vanished after the attack in the Boyd building. I told Mom about Stash. I think she needs help most of all. And Mom said we should try to find her, to get her off the streets. I haven't told Mom yet, but I want her to stay with us. I don't want her to end up in just another foster home.

And Janice? The city paid for her funeral. There was Mom and me, a couple of kids. I think they were in her gang, but I'm not sure. They all kind of looked alike to me. I figured the gang had their own memorial, that night in the graveyard. I think that would be more their style. The reporters didn't bother covering the funeral. Old news, I guess.

There was a lot of coverage of the attack itself in the papers and TV. It seemed Age wanted to send a message to the gangs. Janice had messed around with his plans too many times. The other kids were beaten up, but Janice was the real target.

Right after, the mayor and the premier said they'd be setting up committees, looking into biker gangs and the "plight of street kids" and all that stuff. A lot of big words. Nothing much has happened that I can see. There are still a lot of hungry kids at the shelters. I still see them on the street. Age and three other bikers were arrested. According to the news reports, Age's real name is Alfred James something. No wonder he used a nickname. I told the cops everything I could, but I was the only one. None of the kids would say a word against Age. They all said they didn't know who attacked them. I guess they knew it would be smarter to keep quiet, or they'd all end up like Janice.

I walked by the parkade the other day. They've torn it down to build a fancy new hotel. All that's left is the wall attached to the office tower. It's covered in graffiti. One in particular made me kind of sad. It was the mural of Janice and her gang. The one that made her look like a goth angel. It bothered me that it was out in the open now, for anyone to stare at, or laugh at.

So? What's the big mystery? Why did I decide to start writing a diary?

I got mail from Meghan today. A birthday card. There was a note with it. She says she's in Vancouver, having fun, meeting lots of great people. She told me not to bother looking for her, she'll come home when she's ready. If she ever is. She said she was sorry for what she did. For setting up Janice and the others. That she didn't think it would get that bad. I guess she knew I had figured it out. She said she still thought it was the only way to get away from Age and the others.

I crumpled it up and tossed it in the trash. A perfect 2 points.

Then I thought about Janice, how she told me that on the street we have to watch out for each other. I took Meghan's note back out of the trash, and decided on one thing I have to do after school. I'm going to get a job in Vancouver. I'm going to find Meghan and make her stop playing this stupid game.

I'm going to bring my sister home.

Until next time,

— Kyle